SEVEN TEARS
AT
HIGH TIDE

Seven Tears at High Tide

C.B. Lee

duet. an imprint
of interlude**press**

For anyone who's ever felt they had to choose.

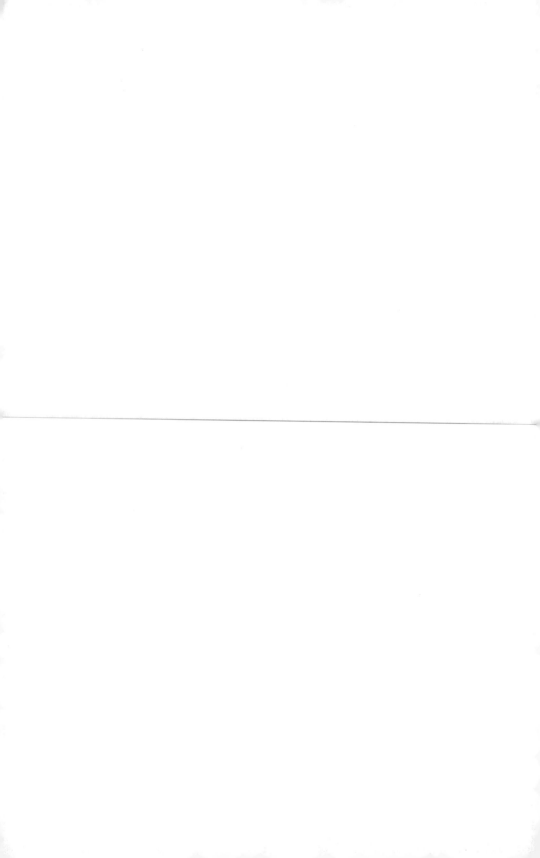

One.

KEVIN KICKS DISTRACTEDLY at the wet sand beneath his feet. Bits of broken seashells and stray pieces of kelp fly up as he goes, but he doesn't bother looking through the debris or even admiring the glint of dark mica in the sand grains. He just keeps walking forward, lost in his thoughts.

The morning is typical June gloom with gray clouds hanging thick overhead, and the water has yet to take on that shimmering azure pictured in all the postcards. In a few hours the clouds will burn off and the sky will be bright and blue; the water will be dazzling, making picturesque waves as it splashes against the rocks by the lighthouse. But for now, dark waves crash onto shore in noisy tumbles of gray-white foam, and water surges up the beach, darkening the white sand.

Kevin takes a deep breath and tastes salt in the wind. Seeing the water extend to the horizon; listening to the sound of the waves tumbling ashore; thinking about how the sea is an inevitability, a constant, as it follows the rhythms of time from ages long past— these things never fail to calm Kevin and fill him with awe. It's a familiar comfort, coming to the beach for quiet contemplation of his place in the universe.

Yet today the beauty of the ocean barely seems to register. Kevin ignores a greeting from a couple holding hands on their morning beach walk, who are chatting excitedly about their trip to Hearst Castle.

Tourists.

The summer brings them out in droves, smelling of sunblock and spreading out all over the beaches in their cars and bikes and RVs. They stop in Piedras Blancas to see the lighthouse and the seals and for the picturesque ideal of the central California coast. Kevin normally doesn't mind all that much, but right now the idea of these happy strangers makes his own misery stand out starkly in comparison.

Today only a few earnest joggers are making their way down the trail along the bluffs; no one else is on the shore now, aside from Sally at the lifeguard tower. Her shift doesn't start for another hour or so, but he knows the college student likes to watch the sunrise and study before the day gets busy. She props her feet up on the sign that reads: "Lifeguard on Duty from 8 AM to Sunset, Swim at Your Own Risk!" and waves at Kevin.

He doesn't have the heart to stop for a conversation so he just nods, hoping she's too far away to see his red and puffy eyes or the dirty tear tracks smudged on his cheek.

He thought this summer would be so different. He and Miles planned to hang out every day, go surfing, play videogames, study for the SAT together. When Miles moved next door in February, Kevin had been sitting on his front porch reading an adventure novel. He was startled out of the story when he heard the moving truck's horn blare, like a herald's announcement. Kevin looked up to see Miles stepping out of the moving truck, and time just seemed to slow. Miles had flipped his blonde curls back and waved hello with a dazzling smile, and it was as if the hero from his novel had come to life.

A guy his age, a *hot* guy his age, who came over that first weekend and wanted to hang out and didn't laugh at watching *The Lord of the Rings*, which was the first thing that popped into Kevin's head when Miles asked him to hang out. Kevin was so distracted by Miles' pretty blue eyes and his jawline he had stumbled over his words, but Miles said yes.

Kevin was nervous throughout the movie, wondering if this counted as his first date, if they should sit closer. Or was that too fast? Kevin started babbling about random neat stuff like the cast filming in New Zealand before he realized he was probably coming off as a huge nerd. But Miles just said, "You're pretty cool," and made Kevin blush hot when Miles bumped his shoulder playfully. Miles was the kind of guy whom the popular crowd courted—attractive and athletic—but Kevin met him first, and they were friends.

It was awesome. Miles didn't seem to mind Kevin's low social status and was grateful for the company on their daily bus rides to and from school. His transfer in the middle of the year meant he was behind in making new friends, and Miles constantly told Kevin how lucky he was to have met him.

It was great, having someone to sit with at lunch, and do homework and watch movies with. And then when Kevin thought it couldn't get any better, one afternoon in late May when they were walking home from the bus stop, Miles kissed him, laughing when Kevin fumbled and attempted to reciprocate. "You like me, don't you?" Miles said.

Miles' words ring through Kevin's head now, but his playful tone has turned mocking. Kevin always liked Miles more than Miles liked him. Kevin was too caught up in the thrill of making out for the first time, too quick to agree they weren't boyfriends, nodding when Miles told him he wasn't ready for that. Kevin thought that, once Miles realized how much the weeks of stolen moments and secret smiles had meant to him, their friends with benefits situation would turn into a real relationship.

But apparently their time together meant nothing, nothing at all.

Kevin wipes away the tears leaking stubbornly from his eyes and walks onto the pier. His bare feet stick wetly to the wooden planks that creak beneath his feet as he heads toward the ocean with the salty wind sharp on his skin. He walks past the surf crashing on the shore, keeps going out where the waves are still growing, to the edge of the pier, where no one, not even the joggers, can see him cry. If anyone notices, they will see a boy sitting on the edge of a singular man-made construction, small against the vastness of the ocean.

It's exactly where Kevin wants to be. He wants to look out into the ocean and feel as if he and his problems mean nothing in the face of the never-ending waves. He wants to feel the inevitability of the tides rolling in and out, of the ocean churning rocks into sand. Being on the beach, watching the rhythm of the ocean has always helped him feel peaceful.

But today the calming view throws into stark relief the turmoil Kevin feels inside. He can't focus on anything but how broken and rejected he feels.

This summer—this was supposed to be ours.

Yesterday afternoon, Kevin walked over to Miles' house, and suddenly everything was different. He had made plans for them, argued with his sister about borrowing her car so he and Miles could drive down to San Luis Obispo and have the whole day to themselves. A theater was showing a Marvel marathon, finishing with the newest movie, and Miles had been excited about it for weeks. They were going to be blissfully alone, and maybe Miles would realize that they were far from school and no one would recognize them, and they could hold hands and kiss and do things regular couples did.

Everyone in their small town knows who Kevin is and that he's bisexual. He's been out since freshman year and never thought he'd have to hide who he dated. Kevin wanted Miles to be comfortable, so he agreed to say nothing about them being together. He figured the movie marathon could be a way for them to have an actual date.

But when Kevin told Miles about the plan, Miles laughed in his face and said, "I don't get where you get off thinking I'm gay, or that I would hold hands with you all day in a movie theater."

"Okay, so maybe bi then, like me, or whatever you are, that's all fine," Kevin said. "I thought you said last week you wanted to go. I got my sister's car tomorrow, and we could totally go—"

"I told the guys on the soccer team I'd go with them to the marathon."

Kevin narrowed his eyes. These were the new friends Miles was so excited to hang out with? The same guys who had made fun of Miles and his thick glasses when he first transferred to their high school?

"Where are your glasses?"

Miles kicked his foot at the air. "Got contacts," he muttered. "Better for sports."

Kevin had to admit that without the glasses Miles' face was even more handsome, but now wasn't the time to be thinking about Miles' eyes. "Okay, how about the day after tomorrow?"

"Uh, that's when summer practice starts, and I really have to get into shape to catch up to all the other guys. Plus I'm not gonna watch it *twice,* just for you."

"What happened to 'I wish we could hang out all the time'?" Kevin asked, thinking about the time he and Miles had been curled up in his bed watching a movie together, hands intertwined. Miles had kissed softly along Kevin's jaw and whispered in his ear.

Miles turned bright red. "That's not—I didn't mean that. Look, we're not a couple or anything. I've just been hooking up with you because you were convenient, okay? I mean, you're pretty cute for an Asian guy, but you talk about rocks too much and… I haven't been doing myself any favors hanging around you at school, never mind if I *dated* you. And I have real friends now, people who count. I don't need you anymore."

"Are you serious?" Kevin asked, frozen where he stood.

"Yeah. You should go. Skylar is picking me up so we can go buy new cleats together."

Sure enough, a car pulled up and Skylar Williams, the richest kid in school and captain of the soccer team, stepped out. He swung his keys jauntily as he walked over and pushed his sunglasses to the top of his head. Kevin had to resist rolling his eyes; everyone at school knew Skylar bragged about going all the way to San Francisco for his fancy haircut, but Kevin has known this kid since the third grade and knew that Kevin's Aunt Lisa has cut his hair once a month since they were both kids.

"I didn't know you knew this loser," Skylar said, giving Kevin a sideways glance.

"We're just neighbors, Sky," Miles said, and Kevin bristled at the familiarity of the tone. Skylar had called Miles a 'four-eyed freak' on his first day of school, and now Miles was giving him nicknames?

"Wow, that sucks," Skylar said. "I can't imagine seeing his stupid face all the time."

The sting of hurt only intensified when Miles said, "I know; it's the worst," and then laughed along with Skylar.

Kevin didn't even have a comeback, just turned tail and ran straight back to his house.

It was difficult to keep his feelings in; he didn't have a valid reason to be sad in front of his family. They didn't know he had been dating anyone. How would Kevin explain that he'd had his heart broken by a boyfriend who had turned out not to be a boyfriend?

Kevin sits on the edge of the pier, dangling his arms and legs through the slats of the wooden rails; bitter tears streak down his face. A thick mist hangs off the horizon, making the sea look ominous. He can't see the oil rigs in the distance because of the cloud cover, so the ocean seems unmarred and fathomless.

The high tide continues to come in; water rushes past the posts. Kevin watches strands of seaweed float by as the waves bob through the tangles and make for the shore. He has a great joke about kelp he planned to tell Miles, but now Miles isn't here, because Miles is a complete jerk who was leading him on the entire time.

A fat tear falls off Kevin's cheek and into the tide.

Good, he thinks. *More salt for the sea.*

Another tear, and then another.

Something Kevin's mother once told him comes back to him, one of her old stories from her childhood in Scotland, something about seven tears at high tide and wishes.

Kevin blinks again. He has nothing to lose by making wishes based on old wives' tales and he lets the tears roll down his face. He counts to seven, wipes his face and watches the tide.

There's no sound but the rush of water churning, the wind blowing through his own hair and the slight creak in the wooden plank when Kevin leans back.

"I just want one summer," Kevin announces. "One summer to be happy and in love. I'm sixteen; I get to be stupid about this. I want to have someone who isn't afraid to hold my hand, who'll make out with me when we watch movies, surf with me, go hunting for rocks with me all summer long, someone who'll like me for me and won't drop me for the 'in' crowd."

A strange sound, like a drawn out bark, comes from below him, breaking the waiting silence.

Kevin looks down.

A seal is in the water; its shiny brown eyes look back at him. Its dappled gray and black fur is shiny and soft-looking, sleek with water. The seal tilts his head at Kevin, as though he's considering, and then spins about in a circle.

A small smile tugs at the corners of Kevin's lips as he watches the seal swim around the edge of the pier, making noises and chasing its tail, disappearing for a bit in the kelp forest and then coming back, as if he's performing. The seal's a bit far from the rookery, but it's not unusual to see them by the pier.

This is the weirdest behavior Kevin has ever seen in a wild seal, and finally he can't help but laugh. The seal barks once more, and it almost looks as if it's smiling in approval.

"Thanks, dude," Kevin calls out to the seal, who just warbles at him and swims along the pier as Kevin starts to walk back to shore.

The seal waves a flipper at him before ducking under an incoming wave, and Kevin loses sight of him under the water.

Oh well. It was an unexpected diversion from what Kevin is sure will be the rest of his terrible, lonely summer.

Kevin is almost at the edge of the dock when he notices someone thrashing in the water, their pale arms barely visible in the incoming wave. It's still early for swimmers. The surfers aren't out yet, and Kevin can tell this guy isn't wearing a wetsuit. The water has to be ridiculously cold, and yeah, he's definitely struggling.

It's a good thing Sally usually gets here before her shift starts. Kevin glances at the lifeguard tower, expecting to see her rushing forward into the waves, but the station is empty. Out of the corner of his eye he spots her in the parking lot, rooting about in the trunk of her car.

It's a quick, immediate decision. Kevin rushes over. Wet sand sinks beneath his toes as he races across the beach and into the surf. The person is only waist deep, flailing, but Kevin doesn't judge; it can be pretty easy to be knocked off your feet. Kevin grasps a hand and pulls him out—a teenager with messy brown hair and a face still round with baby fat. He sits up unsteadily. He's holding something in his other hand, something dark that looks like a wetsuit all folded up. *That's weird. Did he want out of the suit mid-swim?*

Kevin's heart races, but the boy doesn't seem to be injured. In fact, he only seems mildly surprised and looks down at his arms and feet as though he doesn't know what to do with them. He looks up at Kevin and grins, and Kevin is struck by how sunny and bright his smile is and forgets to move. Still holding the boy's hand, he lets the next wave roll in

Water surges around Kevin's body, but he doesn't notice. The boy's sandy brown hair is plastered to his face, and he pushes his hands clumsily at the wet fringe until it's out of his eyes. The morning sun reflects warmly in his brown eyes, on his wet hair playfully tousled by the surf. The next wave pushing past them doesn't seem to faze him. There's a sense of wonder in his eyes, a bright curious joy that radiates outward.

All right. All right. Kevin realizes he's been staring. He lets go of the soft hand, noticing how cold the other boy's skin is.

"Hey, are you okay?" Kevin asks.

The boy nods his head. Water drips from his dark hair, down his face and the hollow of his throat and pools at his bare collarbones. Dimples form in his plump rosy cheeks when he smiles at Kevin, and there's a smattering of light freckles across his nose. He doesn't speak, just looks warmly at Kevin. Shining droplets clinging to his eyelashes catch the morning sunlight, and Kevin has to catch his breath.

"C'mon, you should dry off. You look like you're about to catch a cold." Kevin reaches out his hands again and the boy lets him pull him towards the shore. He stumbles a little, and Kevin holds him steady until they're both out of the water.

Kevin blushes when he realizes the boy is naked and quickly averts his eyes. "Did you lose your swimsuit in the tide or something? Or are you one of those guys who doesn't wear anything under their wetsuits?"

Kevin catches a glimpse of a very nice butt as his new friend turns around and gives the ocean a strange look, as if he expects it to answer Kevin's question.

The boy turns back and tilts his head at Kevin.

"Too cold to answer, I get it." Kevin unzips his hooded sweatshirt and hands it to him. "Here, warm up in this. I'll go see if the lifeguard has, like, a towel or some spare clothes."

The boy sets down the wetsuit carefully by his feet, and then takes Kevin's sweatshirt and holds it delicately in his hands.

"Ugh, you're not even shivering; that means you're too cold to even expend the energy. That's bad." Kevin grabs the sweater and starts tugging the boy into it. It was huge on Kevin, and is clearly much too big for this boy, but at least his junk is covered and he's getting warm. He looks up, wide-eyed, from the hood of the sweatshirt as Kevin zips it up. "Stay here; I'll be right back."

Kevin rushes off to the nearest lifeguard tower, and Sally is back, with her nose in a chemistry textbook and her red windbreaker wrapped tightly around her torso. Kevin explains the situation as quickly as he can, and after Sally apologizes for not being there and thanks Kevin for helping the boy, she lets him take some clothes from the lost and found pile and gives him a fluffy towel.

When he gets back to the pier, the strange boy is gone.

Two.

THE SEA IS a symphony of pleasant noise when Morgan returns; the sounds envelop him warmly as he dives back into the ocean. The water welcomes him, and Morgan can feel a thrum of excitement from the Sea. He throws his pelt over his human shoulders and swims forward, concentrating and calling forth the magic that lives within him. Going back is easier; his pale limbs disappear in favor of flippers, and then all of Morgan's senses are alight again with awareness—of himself, of the Sea all around him.

Did I do right? Morgan asks, sending the hopeful question out toward the ocean's depths.

Even though some selkies say they've heard the Sea's voice, Morgan has never heard it; he's just glimpsed an image or felt a phantom emotion that some selkies might explain away. Morgan believes, though, like his mother and most of his herd, that the Sea is alive, and not just a magical network of information, not just a collection of memories and stories from which selkies can pull knowledge. He's felt the Sea's life, knows that the Sea, after centuries of emotions and dreams and desires poured into it, is a force to be reckoned with.

Morgan is still a bit lightheaded over his encounter. He's never taken the human form, not even as a pup playing at the shift. Unlike most of his brothers and sisters, he'd never had an interest in running around on two legs, playing at being human. Transforming meant something different for Morgan, something he wasn't ready to think about.

Water brushes over him as he swims, and Morgan knows this pleased rush of approval flowing through his body isn't only his own excitement. The Sea is telling him his first transformation went well, and there's no judgment for having waited this long to try it.

Shifting wasn't as difficult as he'd imagined it would be. The transformation, slipping out of the sealskin, came easily, almost as easily as breathing. It wasn't planned, but the boy looked so sad. Morgan wanted to let him know he was listening, that the Sea had heard his Request, and it would be filled. He watched the boy walk back to shore and barked out reassurances, but then realized the human wouldn't be able to understand them.

Transforming took more energy than Morgan had thought it would; he closed his eyes and concentrated, willing his body to change. He held on tightly to his pelt so it wouldn't be lost to the water, but then the wave took him by surprise, dragging him under. Disoriented in the churning water and unable to find his balance, Morgan struggled in the surf.

The boy, *Kevin Luong*, the Sea helpfully reminds him, grabbed his flipper—no, hand—pulling him out of the water to a standing position. Kevin's fingers were solid and warm as they held him steady.

Morgan was fascinated; he had never seen a human so close. Kevin's skin was golden and warm, and he had bright brown eyes that stared back at Morgan with a worried expression. He was saying something, but Morgan was too stunned to understand it, too caught up in watching him, listening to the way Kevin's voice sounded, strange and beautiful, traveling directly through the air.

Then Kevin removed his skin, the bright blue one, and handed it to Morgan. He must have thought him cold and suffering, and the gesture—while not the same for humans, probably—still struck a chord with Morgan. Kevin gave him his skin for safekeeping. Morgan held it carefully in his hands, feeling the soft texture. Why anyone would abandon this beautiful person baffled him.

Kevin shook his head, took the skin and helped Morgan into it, then secured it tightly around him. It was warm and soft and quite possibly the best gift Morgan had ever received. As Morgan worked up the courage to tell him the Sea had heard his Request and it would be fulfilled, Kevin rushed off. Morgan watched him race across the sand, and the next wave of water that curled around his feet—what a new, curious sensation that was— brought with it a reminder from the Sea: It had been a long while since the Sea had received a formal Request.

His family is watching over this area for the summer, he'll be needed, at least for the discussion of the Request and who will honor it. His observations could be helpful. Kevin will need someone who appreciates him, who can make him laugh. His sad eyes are beautiful, and they would surely be incandescent when he's happy.

The voices of the Sea sink into his skin like a comforting touch as he swims north. Morgan picks up speed; he'll probably be lectured for swimming so far away on his own. Morgan has yet to convince his mother that exploring is a worthwhile pursuit, fun, even, and he's not needed on the hunt because their herd has more than enough qualified hunters. Morgan does feel a little guilty, though. He shouldn't have transformed to meet Kevin right after the Request was made, but there's a slim-to-none chance he'll be the one chosen to honor it. He has the least experience with humans of any of the younglings, has never spent any time on land, and has never fulfilled any Request. Morgan still regrets leaving Kevin on the beach without saying goodbye, and realizes that he didn't offer any reassurances. Did he speak at all? Morgan makes a sad, embarrassed noise as he swims, startling a school of fish.

Even if it was a bit awkward, Morgan's glad he didn't pass up the chance to meet Kevin, if only for one moment.

Morgan saw Kevin's heart, as all selkies can, and knew the brightness of his soul and the very core of him, from his stubbornness and impulsive streak to his huge capacity for love and patience. He knew these things in an instant and loves Kevin for them, and now wants to know more than a simple surface reading of his heart can offer.

Morgan swims past the rookery, hearing the familiar barks of his more mundane cousins sunning themselves, indifferent to the packs of humans gawking at them from the cliff above. Morgan strains his ears to hear what they're saying, but he's always found it difficult to communicate with them; *warmwarmsleepsunwarmwarm* is all he's getting from the excited chatter on the rocks. Morgan barks a greeting and tells them the tide is coming in, but they don't understand much more than his hello.

He carries the skin Kevin offered carefully in his mouth as he swims away from the shore. It's a strange texture, and looks different from the golden color of the boy's skin. *Color.* The way the world exploded into a myriad of different hues when Morgan first transformed was overwhelming. The Sea provides names for the colors humans see, and Morgan has the time now to match them to those he's seen. Black, for Kevin's hair. Brown, for his eyes. Blue for the sky and the ocean, looking startlingly different from those he knows, yet still they're blue, beautifully warm shades that change with the wind.

The skin looks different now that he's a seal again. He remembers seeing with his human eyes that it was a vibrant shade of blue, almost purple, like fish Morgan's only seen in tropical waters, and with large slashes of yellow in a pattern across the front. The humans use these patterns to communicate with each other, Morgan knows. The Sea has this information, and the knowledge spills into his head, trickles slowly at first and then floods though. Morgan is a little dizzy with it, but he can interpret what the skin says: *North Cambria High School*. It doesn't mean anything. The Sea's magic is powerful, but Morgan can't expect it to explain all of human culture. He should ask his sisters. They've spent time on land.

The water is slow to warm this morning. Morgan takes a break, treading water as he looks to the cloudy sky. He's been swimming for an hour, his sleek body cutting through the water effortlessly. He thinks about how strange it was to be in human form, the different way the water felt on his skin and hands, how he felt cold and exposed without his fur, how the sounds felt, flat and jarring on his body. The Sea has an explanation for this too, something about sound traveling in water versus air, but Morgan's still a bit lightheaded from the last big piece of information he's absorbed, so he pushes it aside to learn later.

The water carries the sound of a school of fish approaching, and any other day Morgan would be happy to chase them down and make a meal of them, but he's holding something precious in his mouth. He can eat later.

Morgan dives beneath the water, swimming until he can feel the familiar voices of his family talking excitedly; their chatter brushes across his body like a welcome. A wave carries him ashore, and

Morgan's younger brother Dorian waddles toward him, barking excitedly.

"Did you hear the Request? Mother's gathered everyone around to talk about it." Dorian's words tumble together.

"I was there," Morgan says around his mouthful of Kevin's gift. He shuffles over to a nearby dry rock and sets it down carefully, nosing it to make sure it stays out of reach of the high tide.

"What do you mean, you were *there?* What were you doing all the way over there? I heard it was out by the Moon's Eye, where the humans live."

"I was swimming." Morgan shuffles past Dorian, kicking sand at the pup who sneezes and makes a face at him.

"What is this? Why did you steal a human's clothing?" Morgan's older sister sniffs at the blue thing.

"Eat barnacles, Naida," Morgan says, pushing her away. "I didn't steal it. It was a gift."

"From a human?"

Morgan can feel the surprise in her voice; the sound feels different on his skin than it would underwater, but he knows she's about to start pestering him with questions. Luckily, he can hear his mother's voice carry across the shore. "Morgan. You are late. We were waiting for you."

His mother Linneth is in her human form, sitting cross-legged in the sand with her pelt draped over her. The rest of his extended family sits around her in a vague semblance of a circle. Some, like his mother, are out of their pelts, lying in the sand and enjoying the summer sun. Morgan wonders if he should transform as well, but decides not to. He plops down next to his brother Marin. "You could have started without me."

"We really couldn't," his mother says in reply.

MORGAN'S ALWAYS FOUND Council meetings boring. Their herd has always had relatively informal meetings, with everyone welcome to attend, listen and offer input. Their herd is small for selkies, with only thirty-eight of them altogether and seven adults making up the Council. Morgan can't remember many formal meetings—a few Requests, but mostly routine talk about hunting grounds and currents and travel plans, visiting herds they are friendly with, or herds former members have mated into. The most exciting meeting was in his eleventh year when they feared a kraken had come to their territory, but it was just a mistaken report from one overly excited selkie from the south.

Morgan makes a face at his older sister, Naida, who is listening carefully, nodding as the talk veers toward declining herring populations and what that means for the local hunt. Morgan shakes his head. He knows Naida's probably bored too, but she's seeking their mother's approval because she's being considered for leadership. Naida sticks her tongue out at Morgan before replacing the mask of interest and looking back toward Linneth.

Dorian nudges at his side; the pup is yawning already, and Morgan drapes a flipper over him and pets him lazily. His brother makes sleepy, contented noises, and Morgan soon finds himself idly looking around the circle at his family.

He notices his cousin Micah isn't paying attention either, but is caught in a whispered conversation with his new mate, Oki. Oki's only been with the herd since the spring. When they left the icy waters of the north, he came with them to be with Micah. Both of them look quite happy on the beach tonight, curled up with one another in human form, as Oki combs fingers through Micah's blond curls. Micah's arms wrap around Oki's shoulders; his fingers stroke the soft white pelt slung casually over his shoulder. Oki's human form is beautiful, with the broad, flat nose and deep olive skin of the people of the North, and they look good together, laughing softly, lost in their own world.

Morgan isn't very fond of Micah, who's always teased him way too much, but the image of the two of them, young and happy and mated, blossoming in the joy of new love, fills him with a pang of longing.

He wants that, too.

His mother's clear voice breaks through his thoughts. "And lastly, on the matter of Kevin Luong, who lives not far from here, near the Moon's Eye. Kevin has Requested a summer of love and companionship."

Morgan hopes whomever they choose will give Kevin the summer of happiness he deserves. Kevin is a good soul; he should have all the things he Requested, someone to share all those activities. Morgan didn't understand any of them except for the one about searching for rocks, but he's sure one of the other selkies with more human experience will know exactly what Kevin meant.

"This Request will be fulfilled by Morgan."

"What?" Morgan freezes.

Dorian whines underneath him now that the petting has stopped and head butts him to keep going. Morgan puts his flipper back, strokes his little brother's back and tries to process what is happening. Everyone turns to look at him with various expressions— awestruck nods from a few of the younger ones, a stern nod from his grandmother, a surprised gasp from Naida.

Linneth gives him a small, proud smile. "Yes, we've decided you're ready for your first Request. You will do well, I think. The Sea tells me you've already made contact with this Kevin, so I believe this will be easy for you."

"Easy?" Morgan repeats, heart racing. "I've never transformed into a human before today! I don't know anything about

SEVEN TEARS AT HIGH TIDE

them—what if I do it wrong?" *What if Kevin doesn't like me,* Morgan doesn't say, but the fear runs through his body like a cold shudder.

"Do you *want* to take this Request, Morgan?" Linneth walks across the circle to Morgan. Her voice has none of the authority she uses as the leader of the herd, now. It's just an honest question as his mother.

"Yes, I do. I just don't know if I can give him what he needs, all of those things he asked for—the movies and the other things, I don't know—"

His mother smiles at him. "It is enough. I see your nervousness is about wanting to be your best. The little details do not matter; the Sea can help with those. But I can see you already know how you feel about him."

"Oh." Morgan thinks about being in the water by the pier, looking into Kevin's heart, being enchanted by what he saw.

Linneth waits for him to respond, and it takes a moment for Morgan to remember the correct words.

"Yes, I accept this Request, and by the Sea's heart and infinite currents I do pledge myself," Morgan says, feeling the words take power as he speaks them.

* * *

MORGAN DIDN'T EXPECT to be swimming back toward Piedras Blancas with Kevin's sweatshirt after all the care he took to bring it to his family's beach. He'd thought he was just going to keep it safe as a token of a fond memory, but he's going to need it now if he's going to pass as a human.

The morning is calm; waves drift in as Morgan approaches the beach. It's early, and the Moon's Eye stands tall, with its eye closed.

No one is on the beach, so Morgan transforms and walks ashore, holding his pelt and Kevin's sweatshirt delicately.

He recognizes the small building Kevin ran to. A ramp leads up to it. At the top sits a young woman wearing a bright red skin—*no, clothing*, Morgan reminds himself, sorting through the memories and stories he has received from the Sea in a jumble of information. Morgan is proud that he's able to identify the thing in her lap as a book, and is working up the courage to say something when she looks up and blinks at him.

"Holy shit!" she exclaims and stands up.

She appears to be older than Morgan, but younger than Naida. She smells like shock. The odor is somewhat dulled in his human form but he can almost taste the sharp acrid scent.

"Are you okay? You like, lost all your clothes there, dude. Except for that stuff, but bottoms are important too."

"I had a mishap." Morgan shifts his feet in the sand and belatedly holds the sweatshirt and his pelt in front of himself. *Humans are comfortable when they cover themselves,* he recalls. His toes sink into the warm grains, and he tries not to be distracted by the new sensation.

"Went commando in the wetsuit and then came back to find some of your clothes washed away by the surf?" She clucks her tongue. "I'm Sally, by the way. Lifeguarding here for the summer. I'm here mornings, usually. Got a lost and found box filled with clothes you're welcome to—this stuff has been here for ages."

Morgan nods, grateful for Sally's easy acceptance of her own explanation. He walks up the ramp, noting how it creaks beneath his weight.

Sally brings out a box full of clothing and other items Morgan doesn't recognize—shiny, colorful things. He ventures into the box; his eyes are drawn to a bright swatch of fabric, orange, like a tropical fish. Morgan pulls it out, and it smells somewhat familiar.

"Actually gave out some of this stuff yesterday. Kevin found this guy on the beach who lost his stuff too," Sally says, giving Morgan a curious look. "That wasn't you, was it?"

"It was. I am not the most graceful."

Sally laughs, putting away the box now that Morgan's picked something out.

Morgan sets down his pelt and puts Kevin's sweatshirt atop it, then pulls the orange thing up to his waist and keeps the sealskin in his sight. He'll have to find a good hiding spot, somewhere he can—

"Wait, you know Kevin? Kevin Luong?" Morgan asks.

Sally raises her eyebrow. "Yeah, I went to high school with his sister. It's not a big place, Piedras Blancas. You just move here?"

"Yes! Where can I find Kevin? I met him yesterday and would love to see him again."

Sally considers Morgan, tilting her head and looking at him so seriously that Morgan thinks if she were a selkie, she'd be reading his heart and intentions. Maybe she *is*. Morgan smiles at her, hoping she finds him acceptable.

Sally smiles back and points toward the town. "Follow this road till you get to Main Street, make a left on Arroyo Seco. The Luongs live in the blue house at the top of the hill."

"Thank you so much," Morgan says, brimming with excitement and pleased with himself for figuring out this human thing. He even talked to someone and didn't embarrass himself! Well, not too much.

Morgan pulls on Kevin's sweatshirt, reveling in the soft feel of the fabric, and clutches his pelt to his chest. He waves goodbye to Sally and heads down the beach, looking for a good place to hide the sealskin. It will have to be where few humans would go, or could go. Maybe someplace underwater, weighed down by a rock? Morgan considers this and then rejects the idea, not wanting to push his human form to hold a breath longer than needed. But the water idea is good. Maybe a place unreachable at high tide.

Morgan follows the beach, noting on the cliff face the heights high tide will reach, and soon finds himself on a shore studded with rocks worn smooth by the surf. He smiles, looking at all the lovely shades and textures—earthy pinks studded with dark grains, mottled brown stones glistening wet, dark pieces striped with sharp contrasting white, and standing out every now and then, a piece of brilliant green. He already knows: *Kevin would love this*.

Farther down the shore, Morgan finds a cave tucked into the cliff face that will be completely submerged at high tide. He steps inside and touches the cool stone wall. The cave is empty, and Morgan's footprints are the only ones on the soft sand. He can hear the roar of the ocean behind him and the distant echo from the cave winding through the rock.

He tucks his sealskin behind a boulder, secures it so it won't drift away at high tide and stands up, satisfied with the way it seems to disappear into the shadows of the rocks around it. There will be plenty of time to find the perfect hiding place in this cave later. Morgan has a Request to fulfill and someone he has to meet.

Three.

"OBFUSCATE," KEVIN SAYS, reading the flashcard. "Something… something difficult," he mutters to himself, and then flips it over and reads the definition. "Close enough."

His parents are talking loudly in the kitchen. Kevin sighs, looking at them through the window from the backyard. It's a lovely day, the kind that beckons for a trip to the beach. From here, Kevin can see beyond his blue two-story house down to the sparkling ocean, just a ten-minute walk away. So much for the backyard being a non-distracting study environment. He hasn't gotten much done in his room, with his laptop and the endless temptations of the Internet. His rock collection could do with some reorganization and he does have some new specimens that need labeling, which seems infinitely more fun than studying.

But Kevin is trying his best, taking one of the tips from his SAT study guide and sprawling out in the backyard in the grass with his flashcards. He forgot that his parents loved to open all the windows during the day, so their voices carry into the backyard.

"I can't believe Nate emailed you," his dad grumbles.

Kevin's ears perk up in interest. Has someone been hitting on his mom?

"Mike, it wasn't like that." his mom replies. "It wasn't flirty at all. He was asking about you, actually, wondering how we were, how the kids were, whether you've mentioned him. He just seemed concerned that you hadn't responded to his last email. Something important, from the sound of it."

Mike scoffs. "He's sent me three emails in the last week. I can't believe he has the nerve to tell me I should offer him a guest lecture for my summer class, like he'd be doing me a favor. And now he's emailing *you* to bother me about it. Don't believe those rumors that he's on sabbatical, Rachel. I heard he lost his funding and now he's paying for his research out of his own pocket, gone off and taken this bright young graduate student on a wild goose chase—"

The doorbell rings, and Kevin can see his mother pat his father's arm and then go to answer the door.

"Why'd this Nate guy lose his funding?" Kevin calls. Academic gossip is more interesting than his flashcards.

"Ethics violations," Mike says.

Kevin frowns in disapproval. He loves science. This guy deserved to lose his funding if he was doing something unethical. He's about to ask why Nate would be allowed to continue his research independently when his mother comes back into the kitchen.

"Kevin, your boyfriend is here!" Rachel says through the screen door, smiling warmly.

Kevin drops the flashcards, and they scatter all over the grass. His *boyfriend?* Miles must have—he must be here to apologize, to ask Kevin to take him back. A memory of Miles staying for dinner one night, tugging up the collar of his shirt to hide a stray hickey, looking awkwardly at his feet and saying, "No, no, we're just friends" to his parents immediately comes to mind. If Miles told his mom he's Kevin's boyfriend—Kevin's heart beats rapidly, and he jumps up, nearly tripping over the pile of books at his feet. He tugs his hair into place and straightens his T-shirt, just in case.

Kevin races into the house, past his mother, who pats him on the shoulder. "Remember sunblock, sweetie."

It's not Miles standing in the hallway looking at the walls, but the pale boy from yesterday. He's barefoot, wearing a wet pair of baggy orange swim trunks and Kevin's violet-blue school sweatshirt. He's got the hood pulled up and is yanking on the drawstrings until his face is framed.

"Hey." Kevin tries not to sound too disappointed for the boy's sake, as the brief, fragile bubble of hope inside him shatters as quickly as it had formed.

The boy turns, smiling shyly at Kevin.

"I didn't quite catch your name yesterday," Kevin says. "Are you okay? How did you know where I live?"

"Kevin Luong?" His voice has a pleasant, melodic lilt, and he enunciates the words carefully.

"Yeah, that's me." Kevin is growing more curious by the minute. He doesn't remember if he introduced himself yesterday, but it's possible. "Who're you?"

The boy nods and does a funny little dip that might be construed as a bow. "I am Morgan," he says, looking unwaveringly at Kevin. Morgan's eyes are a bright, warm brown, flecked with gold and green.

"It's nice to meet you…?" Kevin is not sure what to do. Morgan stands in the hallway, alternating between smiling at him and looking at the faded peach wallpaper, the paintings on the walls done by Kevin's sister and the shoes scattered in the entryway.

Morgan must have asked around for his address to return the sweater. But he seems to be wearing the sweater quite happily and looks as if he has no intention of returning it.

"Come, it is low tide by the coves now. We can go questing for the rocks you spoke of," Morgan says, extending his hand.

Kevin just stares at him. "Give me a second—I'll be right back." Kevin darts to the living room where his mother is settled on the couch with a stack of essays she has started to grade.

"Mom, why did you say he was my boyfriend?"

She raises her eyebrows. "He was very polite and introduced himself with 'I love Kevin Luong,'" she says, looking at Kevin over the papers in her hand. "I just thought you hadn't introduced him to us yet, sweetie. I'm very happy for you." She sighs. "Ah, young love."

"Mom, I don't—we're not—I only met him yesterday. He got pulled under in a current and I helped him out." Did Morgan really tell his mother that he *loved* Kevin? "I don't even know how he found out where we live."

"That's not too difficult, especially with your name, you know." Kevin must have introduced himself to Morgan.

"I wouldn't worry about it. All anyone has to do is ask where Professor Luong lives," Rachel says. "So the kid has a crush on you after you rescued him. I don't blame him; you're a great catch. What I don't get is why you're still here talking to me when a very cute boy is waiting for you in the hallway."

Okay, so she has a point. Morgan is very cute, even if a little weird. And going back to studying seems very unappealing.

"Fine." Kevin runs to his room and changes into his swim trunks, rubs on some sunscreen and darts back to the front door, where Morgan is crouched, staring at the shoes.

"My family has a thing about shoes in the house."

"So many different adornments." Morgan seems fascinated by the pile of shoes and pokes at the haphazard knots on the laces of Kevin's hiking boots.

"Yeah, we do have a lot of shoes. I should put some of these away; I don't even wear this pair anymore." Kevin shoves aside a pair of old tennis shoes.

Morgan holds his hand out to Kevin as though he's expecting a handshake, so Kevin takes it to be polite, but then Morgan just holds on. His skin is cool to the touch, an unexpected pleasant contrast to the heat of the day.

Kevin blushes and lets Morgan lead him out the door.

"LOOK, I HOPE you don't think this is a date, or anything," Kevin says as they walk toward the shore.

Morgan gives him a strange look. His brown hair looks a lot lighter in the sun, as if it's drying. Was it wet earlier?

He doesn't respond to Kevin's statement, just stares back. Kevin keeps the eye contact, waiting for an answer.

Morgan's round cheeks are starting to pink in the sun; his freckles stand out prominently, scattered generously like stars.

Kevin catches himself staring and decides to break the silence before it gets weird. "All right, I guess not. Why did you tell my mom you loved me? You only met me yesterday."

Morgan shrugs.

"Not really a talker, huh?" Kevin waits for a response, but Morgan is staring at the sky, breathlessly watching a cloud unfurl. It's pretty awesome looking, all light and fluffy, and Kevin doesn't remember the exact name of this type of cloud or he'd try to be impressive. They watch the cloud stretch a little on the wind, until Morgan smiles and looks expectantly at Kevin. Kevin finds himself smiling back and jerks his head toward the trail, and they keep heading forward.

Morgan walks as though he's unsure of his feet, unsteadily making his way down the trail to the shore. Morgan seems fit;

his limbs are compact and thick with muscle, but he seems uncoordinated. He gets better as they continue, and Kevin remembers that when his older sister broke her leg she had a similar stride when she started to get back on her feet.

Morgan is wide-eyed at everything; he pauses to watch a file of ants walk across the trail, plucks a piece of sage and strokes the velvet leaf. Kevin laughs, picks his own piece of sage and breathes in the clean, bright scent. He waves it at Morgan, who steps forward and sniffs cautiously and then inhales deeply.

They get to the shore in good time. It is low tide; the water has receded enough that the various cliffside caves are accessible. The trail is steep, but Kevin knows every step by heart. He grabs Morgan once, twice, a few times to stop him from tripping. Seagulls caw overhead, and the sound startles Morgan, but when he finds the source he laughs and throws his head back; his whole body shakes. The joy is infectious, and Kevin has no idea why the seagulls are so funny, but he finds himself laughing too, especially when Morgan scrunches up his nose and tries to imitate the noise.

They comb the shore side by side. Kevin keeps an eye out for bits of sea glass in addition to any pieces of jade. They're more likely to be found at Jade Cove, but that's an hour north and Kevin doesn't have a car. He hopes they'll find a few good pieces here.

Morgan is good company; he avidly watches Kevin test a rock's hardness by scratching it against his steel pocketknife. "Quartz," Kevin announces happily, showing Morgan the pinkish white stone. Kevin knew it was quartz before he tested it, but nevertheless he feels a thrill of pride when Morgan's eyes widen and he scratches Kevin's knife with the rock until the blade is covered in marks.

"All right, it's not gonna turn into something else while we're holding it," Kevin says, grinning.

Morgan seems to think the test is fun. He picks up every stone and tries to scratch his knife with it. Kevin laughs, surprised at how much fun he's having. Kevin's never had a good time collecting rocks with anyone. His own parents both love hiking and the outdoors, but his dad prefers to spend hours by the tide pools, watching all the creatures within them, while his mom likes to stop to read aloud and would be happy to find a spot to sit and journal. His older sister, Ann, does not like hiking; any nature exploration she does is in her videogames. And Kevin doesn't have any friends his own age to go hiking with. He once tried to take Miles, but Miles complained about Kevin's "stupid little rock collection," and never wanted to come back.

Kevin's used to hiking alone, but having another person here, breathing in the salty air, admiring the view, going at his pace, marveling at the various rocks with him—it's *really* nice.

Morgan turns rocks over, follows behind Kevin companionably, and even listens to him talk about the difference between the Obispo and Paso Robles formations in the bluffs they hike past. When Kevin points out the soft ashy white streaks of volcanic ash embedded in the Obispo siltstone standing out from the younger Paso Robles sediments of earthy clays and sand, Morgan's eyes widen and he says, "Wow."

"Can you imagine what it was like? Volcanoes spewing fire and ash in the air, and all that's left are these memories in the shape of cliffs crumbling slowly to the sea."

Morgan nods.

Kevin has to stop himself when he realizes he's talking a mile a minute, especially when he says, "Looking at a spectacular cliff face is like time travel, to see what the Earth was like millions of years ago, and to touch a stone that has transformed through the ages—it's like magic."

He said as much to Ann when he got really excited on their family vacation to the Grand Canyon, and she just raised her eyebrows and laughed, called him a time-travelling wizard.

"Sorry, you probably think that's weird."

"Oh, not at all." Morgan grins broadly at him and dimples form in his round cheeks. The sun is high in the sky and it looks as though low tide will be over soon. Kevin's bucket is empty; the pickings are slim today, and he's about to ask if Morgan wants to head back to town and get lunch when Morgan finds a piece of jade, wet and shining in a lovely dark green, smooth and worn. He presents the stone to Kevin. "That's a nice one for your collection," Kevin says. "Good eye. Maybe sometime we can head up to Jade Cove sometime; there are a lot of bigger pieces."

Kevin tries to hand the rock back, but Morgan shakes his head. "For you." He presses the stone into Kevin's hand and closes his fingers over it, resting his hand atop Kevin's. The touch is slight but warm, and Kevin hopes he isn't blushing when Morgan moves his hands away. "Thank you," Kevin says, turning over the stone, admiring the color of the embedded jade. He looks up at Morgan, thinking about the gesture and Morgan's invitation to come out here. "How did you know I liked collecting rocks?"

Morgan smiles. "I heard."

"What do you mean, you heard? I'd never met or talked to you before yesterday. Do you know someone from the high school or something?"

There's that smile again.

"What were you doing out in the water, anyway?"

"Swimming."

"Swimming," Kevin repeats. "Is it a habit of yours to swim naked early in the morning?"

Morgan picks up another rock and turns it over in his hands; his long, pale fingers run over the smooth surface. It's another lovely piece, a darker stone with a white vein of quartz running through it. He hands it to Kevin with a smile, then bends to look at more rocks.

"Thank you." Kevin drops the stone in his bucket. "You didn't answer my question. I'm not judging you or anything, if you do like to, um, swim naked." Kevin's cheeks heat up—oh no, he just looked over at Morgan's backside again. Kevin forces himself to stare at the stratifications on the cliff face and tries to push all thoughts about bare wet skin from his mind.

Morgan laughs and he turns and gives Kevin a look that Kevin interprets as, "*Yes, I do. So what?*"

All right, well, that's answer enough. Kevin gets uncomfortable when people make fun of his hobbies. Kevin still reorganizes his rock collection based on whether or not two specimens would get along, a habit from when he was a kid and imagined all rocks had secret, silent conversations with one another. Kevin has no intention of making fun of Morgan's hobbies. So Morgan's an endurance swimmer in training. And a naturist. Maybe. "But you are new in town," Kevin says, hoping to get some information.

"Yes, my family just moved to the area."

Kevin nods, satisfied. "Hey, do you wanna check out that cave?" An opening in the cliff face farther up the shore fills up at high tide, but right now would be a perfect time to explore it. He hasn't made it this far on his own, has never felt brave enough to venture in alone, but right now seems like a good time.

Morgan follows Kevin. They duck inside the rock opening, and Kevin blinks and waits for his eyes to adjust. The sand beneath his feet is still damp, and the air is cool here in the shade, ripe with possibilities. Kevin doesn't know how far the cave goes, but he wants to find out.

The cave echoes with their footsteps and the *drip drip* of water trickling steadily from the walls.

"Wow, look at this!" Kevin pauses to look at the reddish brown clays and lighter, nutty golden streaks of sediment slashing across the cave wall, turning his head to admire the angle of the striations. "I wonder if we're inside a small fault."

Morgan touches the wall. "A fault?"

"You know, like plate tectonics, a huge crack in the rock where there's been movement over time."

Morgan nods. "Ah, there is a place underwater where the land slowly grows, moving apart."

"Yeah!" Kevin says, tracing where the red-brown grains meet golden with his fingers. "Underwater diverging plates are really cool. I've seen pictures. I want to study geology in college," he adds. "What about you? Do you know what you want to do?"

"Fish."

"Marine biology is cool, too," Kevin says. "My dad teaches it at Cal Poly. It's really awesome. He's studying sustainable fishing practices and the local marine ecosystems. You could probably ask him stuff about it sometime. I'll introduce you."

Morgan grins, and something warm and pleasant flutters nervously in Kevin's chest. He wasn't expecting to like the guy. Kevin doesn't have experience with people crushing on him; it still seems unbelievable, as if he's waiting for the other shoe to drop and for Morgan to announce it was a joke. Hanging out with Morgan was more interesting than studying for the SAT, and the nice thing would be to get to know him, maybe figure out why he likes Kevin, odd as that is. Morgan seems so *nice* and down to earth, and he actually seems to—

Something out of the corner of Kevin's eye catches his attention. At first he thinks it's a wetsuit someone left behind tucked behind a loose boulder, but then he steps closer and runs his fingers along the edge and finds it's sleek fur, still slightly damp with saltwater.

Kevin wants to take a closer look, but Morgan says, "The tide is starting to come in." His voice is tinged with fear. He grabs Kevin's hand, interlacing their fingers.

"Right, we should get out of here." Kevin allows himself to be pulled out of the cave.

Kevin's had a lot more fun than he expected on this outing and decides to take Morgan to the cafe on Main for lunch. It's good timing: no tour buses are offloading tourists heading to Hearst Castle. Other than a family in one corner and a small group of hikers huddled in a booth, the cafe is empty. The hikers whisper intently to one another and have topographic maps and photos of seals from the rookery sprawled out over their table. Kevin raises his eyebrow at the amount of hi-tech gear they all seem to have: expensive, moisture-wicking fabrics; top-of-the-line backpacks and trekking poles and what seems to be a lot of navigational equipment.

The hikers seem to be on an elaborate scavenger hunt—geocaching, probably. Kevin's tempted to ask if they're geologists when he recognizes a Brunton compass, an expensive piece of technical field equipment not meant for casual orienteering. But he's more interested in hanging out with Morgan, so he ignores the hikers.

Kevin leads Morgan to his favorite booth by the east window and asks him to wait while he gets them an order of fish and chips to share. Morgan seems to be fascinated by everything in the cafe; he's slowly taking in all the decorations and cheap fishing memorabilia on the walls, the faded photographs and news clippings about the town and especially the people enjoying their food. Morgan avidly watches the family eating together in the corner and listens to the children laugh as they watch a cartoon on a tablet. Kevin can't help smiling when he sees Morgan watch the toddler flick from a cartoon to a game.

A bell chimes from the front counter and Kevin thanks Sue, the owner; he ignores the eyebrow waggle she throws at Morgan waiting for him in the booth. He brings the tray to the table; steam rises from the seasoned food. Kevin sets it down and gestures at it all, but Morgan just watches, staring reverently at the bounty until he makes the first move.

Kevin goes for the French fries, relishing the taste of hot oil and crisp potato. "Here you go." He nudges the tray toward Morgan, who picks up a piece of fish and sniffs it. Kevin gives him an encouraging look. Morgan seems as if he's taking his time to catalogue every part of this experience. "It's good, promise."

Morgan takes a bite of the fried fish, then groans happily around the mouthful. "I've never had fish like this before," he says after swallowing.

"Your family strict on junk food?"

"We eat everything fresh." Morgan takes another bite with his eyes glazed over.

Kevin chuckles and pushes the small dish of tartar sauce at him. "Here, try it with this." He picks up a piece of fish and dunks it generously in the sauce and eats, finishing the piece quickly and then wiping the grease off on a napkin.

Morgan copies him, and then his eyes widen as he chews slowly, clearly savoring the taste.

"French fries," Kevin says, nudging the plate toward Morgan. "And ketchup," he adds, setting the ketchup dish in front of him. Morgan pops one fry into his mouth, makes a satisfied happy noise, grabs a handful and dips each one in ketchup and then stuffs his face, one fry after the other. "Slow down there," Kevin says, laughing.

"It's so good," Morgan mumbles with his cheeks full. A fry dangles from his mouth; ketchup is smeared on his cheek.

Watching a guy eat shouldn't be this endearing, but somehow it is. The way Morgan dives right into trying new food, enjoying every bite, eyes sparkling with exhilaration, is refreshing, and Kevin wonders what other types of food he could introduce Morgan to, just to see him enjoy it.

Kevin grabs a napkin. "You're a mess." He takes Morgan's chin gently. Morgan goes still and lets Kevin wipe his cheek. "Good food?"

"The best," Morgan says.

Kevin realizes he's still very much in Morgan's space. He scoots back, blushing.

"Your mom cooks super healthy or what?"

"My mother," Morgan says slowly, his Adam's apple bobbing as he swallows, "my mother insists we h—"

"Oh, ice cream! Dude, you should have some while you're out, if your family is strict on food." Kevin jumps up, eager to treat his new, sheltered friend, dashes to the counter and orders the house special—a large ice cream sundae with all the toppings.

Sue winks at him as he waits at the counter, bouncing impatiently. "I'll bring it out to you boys; go ahead and sit back down."

Kevin gives her a grateful smile and turns around, only to bump into a solid mass—one of the hikers, an older man, whose face is twisted in a frown. "Watch where you're going."

"Sorry." Kevin throws his hands up in the air, backing up.

The man mutters something as he slides an empty table over to join his group. His two companions, a black woman with her nose buried in a book and a redheaded man typing away on a laptop, look up.

"Well? The summer is only so long, get a move on," the old man says, folding his arms. The other two quickly spread out more maps, and Kevin glimpses coordinates on the laptop screen as he passes by.

"You guys on a scavenger hunt or something? We don't really get a lot of geocachers here," Kevin says, trying to be friendly.

The woman gives him a small smile, but before she speaks the redhead says, "Get lost, kid."

The old guy glares at Kevin. "This is science, not some *scavenger hunt.*" He spits the words out as if they're not worth the breath to say them.

"Whatever." Kevin's got ice cream on its way and Morgan to hang out with; he doesn't need the approval of rude strangers. He settles back into the booth to find that Morgan's finished all the food.

"You're gonna love this," Kevin says, tapping his fingers cheerfully on the table.

Morgan leans back in his chair and stares at the empty plate, looking sated and also slightly embarrassed that he finished the meal. "I finished all the food gift that you shared with me."

Kevin waves him off. "No worries, you can get me next time."

Morgan beams. "Yes, I can definitely bring you a food gift—"

"Order eighty-seven, house special," Sue says, approaching their table.

"Thank you," Kevin says. The sundae looks glorious: nuts and cherries on whipped cream, rivulets of chocolate and caramel sauce cascading down three scoops of chocolate, vanilla and strawberry ice cream.

"Whoa," Morgan says, eyes widening.

"You and your date enjoy, sweetie," Sue says and places two spoons on the table.

Kevin can feel his face turn red. "Um—"

Morgan is already digging in, not paying any attention to the statement. He looks completely relaxed, spooning mouthful after mouthful of the dessert. "This is the best food gift anyone has ever given me."

"I'm glad you like it." Kevin plucks a maraschino cherry off the sundae and plops it into his mouth. "My mom likes the healthy stuff, too, but she doesn't mind me pigging out every now and then."

"Your mother and you are different looking." Morgan is blunt, but curious. His voice lacks the tone of condescension Kevin is used to hearing when people ask about his family.

"Yeah, it's pretty obvious I'm not white," Kevin says, rubbing the back of his neck. He spots his reflection in the shiny chrome napkin dispenser: a blurry Chinese guy with floppy black hair and skin tanned from days spent on long hikes looking for rocks. "My dad remarried when I was four; she's always been Mom to me."

Kevin loves Rachel and has fond memories of growing up with her and his dad, but sometimes he wonders what his birth mom was like. In the living room is a slightly yellowed photo of his family when he was a baby and another black and white photo of his birth mother on the mantle. Kevin has sometimes wondered how he was supposed to grieve for someone he doesn't quite remember. His father and Ann had a more difficult time of it, but Kevin only has stories of her, what she was like. "My birth mom died when I was a baby."

"Oh." Morgan pats Kevin's hand. "I am sure both of them love you very much."

"YOUR MOM TELLS me you went on a date." Mike waggles his eyebrows.

"Dad," Kevin says, rolling his eyes.

"How'd it go? Do I need to give you the talk? Do you have any questions about—I did my research, you know," he says, smiling. "If you need anything, I can get you—"

"Dad, I'm not, we're not—" Kevin starts, horrified that this conversation is taking place.

His parents were nothing but supportive, perhaps a little over-zealous, when he came out to them in freshman year. He came home from school the next day and found pamphlets on everything from peer resources to guidelines on safe sex, and his mother had even purchased him "magazines." It was such a waste of good masturbatory material, too, since Kevin just couldn't get it out of his head that his parents had bought him *porn.*

His mom also bought herself a "PROUD OF MY LGBT KID" sticker for her car and his dad began wearing a rainbow pin everywhere. They even started a support group for other parents of LGBT youth when they found out there wasn't one in their small town. Kevin hadn't planned on being out at school, not just yet, but then Mrs. Williams ran into his mom at the grocery store and she was wearing her PFLAG pin, all proud of her bisexual son, and, well, Skylar Williams threw him in a trashcan the next day.

Kevin loves his parents, even if their eagerness to support him has meant he was out sooner than he expected. But he's had way too many awkward conversations with his dad about sex to want another one.

"You don't need to get me anything. We're just hanging out. It wasn't a date."

"Sue tells me you two shared a sundae and looked pretty cozy," Rachel chimes in.

"The two of you." Kevin shakes his head and heads to his room.

"Awww, our little boy is all grown up and falling in love," Mike says.

"I'm not in falling in love!" Kevin yells down the stairs, and he can actually hear his parents giggling. He shakes his head fondly as he enters his bedroom and puts the bucket on his desk. *Morgan was right: They do love me very much.*

He pulls the stones from the bucket and starts to polish them, whistling as he does.

FOUR.

MANY THINGS ABOUT being a human take a while for Morgan to get used to: the way his body needs to balance itself when he walks, the way sound isn't a feeling, the whole way the world looks. The way the human eye sees colors is one of the most interesting things; so many different shades appear in abundance, everywhere. It's all dazzling and beautiful.

Some of his abilities as a selkie cross over to his human form as well: the acute sense of smell by which they can recognize one another out of the water and sense emotions. It's so interesting, the clouds of contentment and exhaustion and joy and hunger and excitement that float around the humans Morgan has interacted with. The most interesting is Kevin, of course, who still carries an underlying scent of loneliness and dejection, but there were many moments during their outing when he smelled of nothing but interest and a quiet, flourishing happiness. Morgan is pleased that he seems to be doing well in providing Kevin the companionship he asked for in his Request.

The best part about human culture is the food. It's so different, so strange. The first time Kevin gave him a food gift, Morgan's whole perspective changed. He still enjoys snapping fish right out of the water, fresh and raw, but the fried food was so *delicious*.

Morgan doesn't normally hunt this long if he's on his own and not part of the hunting party tasked with bringing food back to the herd. He would usually only eat his fill and move on, but today he's determined to return Kevin's favor. He swims, finding relief in returning to the water as a seal, listening for schools of fish. The Sea welcomes him back; the old collective magic of the depths offer encouragements. A wealth of knowledge flows here, centuries of stories and spells and emotions fed to the oceans, dreams and hopes and desires.

Morgan should probably consult how previous Requests were filled and learn more from the Sea about the human world. But there is only so much transference; the gift of language and understanding is inherent, but many details don't cross over in translation. The Sea understands emotion better than mundane, concrete facts; Morgan knows Kevin is lonely, knows about what he wants and what he fears, but he doesn't understand some of the things he talks about.

It's fine. Morgan learns best by doing, anyway. He learned to swim this way, throwing himself into stronger currents than his mother allowed. She worried, but Morgan figured it out eventually. The same with hunting: Because he was the only halfling, the herd always babied him, but Morgan works hard to be a useful member of his family.

He's an excellent hunter. There's no one to show off to now, but Morgan is diligent, concentrating on getting as many fish as he can. He's ruthless, grabbing one fat fish after another and tossing them in a pile of seaweed. Unsure what Kevin will like, he gets a variety. By the time the sun comes up, Morgan has a formidable, twitching pile of fish and he's never been more proud.

Morgan wraps the food gift in the prettiest pieces of kelp he can find. He almost wants to show this bounty to his cousin Micah, who's always rubbing it in his face that he's a poor excuse for a selkie. Morgan snorts. He bets this is more fish than Micah has ever caught at a time and tries to imagine his poor cousin's expression when he realizes the poor halfling is a better hunter than he'll ever be.

Being a halfling is not something for which Morgan is often teased in the selkie community. Over the generations there have been a few halflings, children born to selkies and humans, some who met through Requests and others by chance. He knows he's the first in a long, long while, and he doesn't know much about his human father, except that he'd done the disgraceful thing and stolen his mother's pelt, hiding it from her, trapping her in her human form in hope of keeping her forever.

Morgan remembers asking about his father, but it always seemed to make his mother sad. Despite the stoic face she presents to the rest of the herd there is always an undercurrent of loss in the awe-filled stories—exaggerated, Morgan's sure—of finding her pelt and stealing away with it, pregnant and triumphant in the middle of the night, then returning to the Sea where she belonged.

With Morgan, she's never used the same language the herd does, never called his father a cruel kidnapper or a grubby mudwalker. Whenever he came to her with questions, her mood changed and she would look out toward the Sea. Eventually she would kiss Morgan on the forehead and tell him not to worry about it. Morgan learned quickly to stop asking.

Did she love his father? Does she miss him? Does she wish their story had ended differently?

Morgan shakes himself. It won't do to put himself into that sad, curious mood about his parents. He focuses on admiring how lovely his food gift looks all wrapped up and tucks another piece of kelp securely around it.

"You should do a bow," says a voice behind him; the familiarity of it is soft on his skin.

"A what?"

"Humans totally do it on their presents." Naida flicks a piece of kelp at him. "I should know; I spent a good year on land."

Morgan doesn't need reminding; Naida flaunts her knowledge of human culture every chance she gets, choosing to speak as they do all the time, which is annoying, since the Sea has little information on the specifics of human vernacular.

Morgan is tempted to ask her about this bow, but he doesn't want to give Naida the satisfaction, so he scrunches up his face. "What are you doing here? I'm on my way to shore."

"Yeah, yeah, you have a Request, chosen by the Council, blah blah blah." Naida flips over onto her back and swims in lazy circles around Morgan. "I mean, I'm the one with more experience with humans. Even Micah's spent more time with them than you. I can't believe they picked you. I mean, not that I don't think you're lovable, little brother, but I really don't think you can pull this off. You don't know anything about being human. I'm kind of surprised, you know, with you being half and all."

"Well, I'm learning." Morgan tugs his package of fish closer to himself and swims away from his sister. He's closer to Naida than to his other siblings. She never brings up the difference in their heritage, and that she's done that now so casually hurts him more than he wants to admit.

Morgan's tried his whole life to avoid shifting like the others, who change on a whim between seal and human as if it was a game, or even like Naida, who spends months at a time on land masquerading as human, even spending an entire year with them.

He's always been painfully aware of his status as halfling; although his mother takes care to treat him the same as all the other children she's had over her years, there's a very obvious gap in age that will always remind the herd where Morgan came from, and what it cost them while their leader was absent for years, trapped as a human. Naida and the older brood are all at least ten years older than he; Dorian and the younger pups are about ten years younger. His mother was reluctant to take another mate after she returned, but she had to take the diminishing herd numbers into consideration.

Morgan's tried all his life to prove that he has a place in the herd, proving that he is a fantastic swimmer, a good hunter and a watchful member of those who live in the Sea. He's curious, sure, but has kept his interest in the human world well under wraps. He doesn't want to seem less of a selkie.

But it's apparently worked to his disadvantage, since his lack of knowledge might keep him from doing well with Kevin's Request.

Naida's expression softens, and she shifts into her human form, grabs a piece of kelp and ties it attractively around his package. "Here. This is a bow." She pushes it back at him and pats his cheek. "You didn't let me finish. I meant I don't think you can pull this off without my help."

"Thank you for the bow." Morgan tries to take the package back, but her hands have a better grip than his flippers, so he shifts as well, then pulls the fish toward himself. His pelt hangs loosely around his shoulders, and it seems precarious and unsafe, as though it might get swept away with an oncoming wave.

Naida doesn't seem to have that worry, her pelt having already fallen off in the scuffle. They laugh as they pull back and forth; her sealskin bobs casually in the water next to them.

"Let go," Morgan says. "This is a gift for Kevin."

"This is a gift for Kevin," Naida mocks, and then she does let go, causing Morgan to fly backward, splashing as he hits the water.

Naida laughs as Morgan flails, trying to regain his balance.

"Your skin!" Morgan calls out in a panic as it starts to drift away on a retreating wave.

Naida swims swiftly after it, catching up to her pelt easily and then shifts back without a blink of an eye. She head butts him playfully. "Aw, you're so cute when you worry."

"Aren't you afraid you'll lose it?"

"Not here." Naida gestures at the open water around them. "On land, though, I've had a few close calls." She laughs again, as if the idea of losing her sealskin is exciting, nothing more than another story to impress the other selkies.

Morgan shifts back into a seal, feeling more comfortable in this body. He can't imagine losing this ability.

"Hey, so bows aren't the only human thing I know about," Naida says. "C'mon, let me swim with you to shore and I'll tell you everything there is to know about humans. What have you two done so far? Have you gone on a date?"

"What is that?" Kevin's said that word a few times, but Morgan is pretty sure Kevin doesn't mean it as a specific day of the year. The first time they walked down to the cove together to look for rocks, Kevin wanted to be very specific that it wasn't a date, but then at the food place someone else thought it was. He explains all of this to Naida, who, to his surprise, listens intently without offering any teasing comments.

"It sounds like he wants to be friends," Naida says, humming thoughtfully. "That's all fine. You can still fulfill the conditions of the Request—this Kevin only wanted someone to spend time with whom he *could* love. Besides, humans think about these things differently than we do. It's a little complicated."

"Yeah." Morgan sighs, thinking of Kevin's face when he told him he loved him.

"It'll work out, Morgan. Look, a date is what humans call it when two people spend time together and they are both interested romantically in each other. People can do lots of different things, like eat food together, or watch movies."

Morgan blows bubbles in the water irreverently, shaking his head. "We walked together and collected rocks. He likes those. And we've eaten food together." They should be doing all the things Kevin mentioned in his Request—and one of them was to watch movies with someone. Movies are something Morgan definitely has yet to do with Kevin. "So what are these movies?"

Naida giggles. "Oh, they're brilliant. I miss them. I totally would come ashore and see if I could sneak into a theater or something, but Mother said specifically no one but you is allowed on land. Something about us bothering you on your Request, making fun of you and stuff." Naida does a glib little flip, flicking water at Morgan.

"I have no idea why she made that rule," Morgan says dryly. "It's not like you guys ever make fun of me."

Naida ignores him, sighing wistfully. "It's fine. I don't think there's a theater in town anyway." She swims idly next to him, talking excitedly about some human quest to destroy a ring and it all sounds very complicated and it's really not helping Morgan at all.

"You still haven't explained what a movie is. All you've been doing is talking about this Aragorn person," Morgan huffs.

"Oh! Right, right. Well, humans have recorded these stories, kind of like how we tell each other stories, but they've also got this magic that lets you see it happen! You'll have to tell me if you watch any of those."

Morgan swims with Naida as she starts telling him how amazing it is, how the moving pictures and the stories come to life. Soon she is talking more about this lord who has many rings and then other movies she saw when she was on land. Naida segues easily into her adventures, going off on tangents about the friends she's made, foods she's eaten.

Morgan is still a little worried that Kevin doesn't want to date him, and that Kevin not loving him will result in him not fulfilling the terms of the Request. This is the first time he's been given an assignment, and he means to see it through. Selkies are supposed to be able to bridge the world of the Sea and the world ashore, to be able to interact with humans and remind them that magic still exists in the world. To fulfill a Request is a high honor, knowing it carries this old purpose of bridging the two worlds for only this brief time. Successfully completing a number of Requests ensures a selkie herd the goodwill of the Sea—good hunting, swift currents and peaceful waters. And if they don't, there are stories, too, of monsters in the depths leaving the dark and the deep, venturing into the shadows to prey on selkies and other sea creatures alike—the kind of beast that could eat a whale and still have room for more.

And that's not counting the weather or other atrocities the Sea could throw at them.

Morgan is more than a little lost in his thoughts when Naida notices his glum mood as she swims. She bumps him. "All right, I'm boring you, what's up?"

Morgan glances skyward, confused. "Clouds?"

"It's a human thing." Naida laughs at him, flicking him on the nose. "I mean, what are you thinking?"

Morgan tells her about his fears, about whether or not Kevin will ever love him back, but Naida reassures him.

"It doesn't work that way. You loving him and being there for him this summer, that's fulfilling the Request. Him loving you back? It's not part of the story, brother."

Naida swims silently with him, and Morgan doesn't mention the sorrow at the edge of her words. She's told lots of stories about her time on land, but sometimes Morgan senses that the couldn't-care-less attitude is an act, and something happened, something that broke her heart.

"Good luck, Morgan," she says as they near the shore. The sounds of people swimming and talking echo in the distance. Naida flips her tail and swims again, leaving Morgan alone with his thoughts.

He swims to the cove, relieved no one is ashore. He shifts; the morning sun is warm on his bare skin as he walks into the cave. In the hiding spot—a better one than the first, farther into the cave—he finds the clothes that Kevin gave him. Morgan folds his pelt neatly and tucks it next to the blue sweatshirt. He considers wearing the sweatshirt again today, but it's fairly warm and he doesn't want to lose it, should he have to remove it to remain cool. *Human bodies are so strange.*

Morgan dresses quickly in the shorts, grabs his kelp-wrapped bundle and makes his way toward Kevin's home.

FIVE.

THE NEXT DAY Kevin keeps busy; he's got chores to do. He watches jealously as his sister reads in the cool shade of the porch awning while he sweats, pushing the lawnmower across the lawn in the summer heat. The marine fog layer burned off early in the morning, and now it's nothing but hot, blaring sunshine. Kevin wipes his brow and adjusts his hat, then grunts as he pushes the lawnmower around a tree.

After mowing there's weeding, and Kevin is up to his knees in the flowerbeds with sweat dripping down his face. He rubs at his eyes and makes a face at the dirt he smudges on himself. *Gross. Whatever, that's what showers are for.* It's not as if he's going anywhere.

Kevin is yanking furiously at a stubborn strand of goosegrass when a shadow falls over him. "Thanks, Ann, stand right there, it's perfect," Kevin says.

He looks up and Morgan is smiling down at him; his sister is still on the porch, eyeing them. She flips her long braid over her shoulder and pretends to read her book.

"Hi, Morgan," Kevin says, standing up. He brushes the dirt off his clothes, feeling self-conscious about the dirt and sweat stains, not to mention his old Power Rangers T-shirt.

"Kevin," Morgan says brightly. Even though he's wearing the same board shorts, he looks clean and put together, ready for the beach with his pale chest bare. Morgan wiggles his toes in the grass. He's holding something. It looks like a huge tangle of seaweed with a longer strand of kelp tied clumsily around it, but Kevin can see something silver and sparkling inside the bundle. "I have brought you a food gift."

"Really?" Morgan holds out the bundle of seaweed, and Kevin unwraps it carefully, grinning as he undoes the first piece of kelp. "Hey, is this a bow?"

Morgan's smile widens and he bounces on the edge of his feet. "Yes! A bow. For the gift."

"Cool." Kevin pulls the 'wrapping' off. The bundle is filled with shiny fish; he recognizes mackerel and snapper in the top layer. "Wow, thanks! Did you catch all these?"

Morgan puffs out his chest. "I'm good at hunting."

It's a weird way to talk about fishing, but Kevin shrugs it off. He takes the still-wet bundle into the house, careful to not drip on the carpet as he makes his way to the kitchen with Morgan following behind him, humming happily.

"What's all this?" Mike asks.

"Morgan went fishing and brought this for us," Kevin says, placing all the fish in the sink. He untangles the last of the seaweed and shakes some of it playfully at Morgan. "Nice wrapping."

Morgan makes a face and dodges the seaweed. Kevin realizes belatedly his dad is just watching them with an amused look. "Oh, Dad, this is Morgan. Morgan, this is my dad, Mike Luong."

"It's very nice to meet you, sir." Morgan bobs his head and smiles.

"Oh, you're a polite one," Mike says, patting Morgan on the shoulder. "Just call me Mike. It's a pleasure to meet you. Thank you for all the fish. I think we can definitely cook these later this afternoon. You're welcome to join us, of course. I just love an excuse to use the deep fryer."

"I love Kevin," Morgan says without missing a beat.

Mike laughs and claps Morgan on the shoulder. "Great, I do too. Kevin has to finish his chores, though. But he did tell me you were interested in marine biology! I'm always happy to talk to someone who wants to go into the field."

Kevin groans. "*Dad.*"

"All right, all right." Mike throws up his hands. "Chores before boyfriend, remember, Kevin. Morgan, you're welcome to hang out. I'm just working on this syllabus if you want to talk about sustainable fishing practices—"

"Friends, Dad, didn't I tell you…?" Kevin looks at Morgan in an embarrassed panic, but Morgan doesn't seem to notice his father's use of the word *boyfriend.*

"I can help Kevin with the chores," Morgan announces. "I love him."

Mike raises his eyebrow and makes a show of whispering to Kevin. "This one's a keeper," he says with a wink. "Just don't let him do all the work. They're your chores for a reason, you know. Builds character."

"Okay, Dad," Kevin says, before he gets wrapped into a conversation about his dad immigrating to America and working hard his whole life. He loves and respects his dad and his history, but Kevin has a suspicion that Morgan's curiosity and willingness to listen will lead to hours and hours of story time.

Kevin grabs Morgan's wrist gently and leads him back outside. "You can't just say things like that."

"Like what?"

"Like that you love me. It's weird. We hardly know each other."

"But I do love you."

Kevin stares at him, slightly annoyed. He doesn't feel like discussing this right now, or getting into the complexities of like versus love and what's too soon and what's not; he doesn't want to hurt Morgan's feelings, not while they're getting to know each other. It's too hot, and he's got tons more gardening work to do. "Look, are you sure you want to help with the weeding? It's not that I don't appreciate it, it's just a lot of hard work, you know, and you don't have to. You can always come back later. We'll fry up some fish and hang out then."

"Fried?" Morgan's eyes light up. He looks at Kevin, clapping his hands together.

"Yes, fried," Kevin says, laughing.

"I would love that. And if helping you with the chores means we can do the fried fish quicker, I'd be glad of it." Morgan beams at him, as if the prospect of getting down in the dirt with Kevin and pulling weeds for an hour is the most fun idea in the world.

Later, at dinner, it's clear that Kevin's family has taken an instant liking to Morgan, especially his dad. It probably has something to do with how appreciative Morgan is of the food. He goes out of his way to compliment the chef.

"Oh, I don't get much chance to cook, so really, thank *you*," Mike says, beaming.

Morgan even laughs at Kevin's kelp joke. Rachel wanted to know why there was seaweed in the sink, and Kevin explained it was Morgan's idea of wrapping paper. "Oh wait—I have this great joke. Okay, okay—where does seaweed go to look for a job?"

Ann rolls her eyes, paying attention to her food, and his parents look on with mild interest.

"The kelp wanted ads!" Kevin finishes proudly.

Morgan laughs, even though his face looks confused. "Why would the kelp need to be employed?"

"It's not—it's a play on words, see? You know, help-wanted, kelp-wanted," Kevin explains.

"Oh." Morgan nods, even though he still looks uncertain. "That *is* very funny."

"He's a huge nerd," Ann teases. "Don't get him started on the rock jokes."

"What rock—"

Kevin's parents and Ann all groan in unison, and Kevin whispers to Morgan, "It's okay, I can tell you the rock jokes later." He's pleasantly surprised when Morgan nods as if he actually wants to hear all of Kevin's jokes.

"Are you and your family visiting for the summer, Morgan?" Rachel asks.

"Yes," Morgan says, eating a piece of fried fish. "I've never been here before. I know my mother visited a long time ago, before I was born, but our family hasn't come back since. It's a beautiful place."

"Piedras Blancas is lovely," Mike agrees. "We've lived here for quite some time. The tourist season can get a bit hectic, but the view and the people are worth it. The rookery's quite pretty too; have you two been up there?"

"Oh, that's where all the seals are," Kevin says. "We could check it out sometime if you like."

Morgan shrugs; seals probably are boring to him. "Whatever you think will be fun," he says, giving Kevin a small smile. "Hiking, rock collecting, surfing, whatever you want."

"Morgan, where are you from?" Ann asks.

"My family travels a lot, but we usually go back to *Arcaibh*."

Kevin doesn't know where that is, but it sounds pretty when Morgan says it, like a chiming bell.

"Oh, you speak Gaelic!" Rachel says. "My mother always tried to teach me, but I could never get the accent right. I've only been to the Orkney Islands once, but they're quite beautiful. All of Scotland is gorgeous, really."

"You've traveled quite a long way," Mike remarks.

Morgan shrugs. "We move around every year. My mom is a representative of…" He trails off, looking uncomfortable.

"Oh, a diplomat's kid," Rachel says. "I know how that feels. I don't think I've really settled at all, even since I grew up. At least until I married Mike and we moved here," she says, and Mike kisses her on her cheek. "We met on a beach, you know."

Kevin and Ann share a look.

"It was right after I got tenure," Mike says, a dreamy look in his eyes. "I signed up to teach a unit for this experimental field expedition that Rachel had helped put together."

Kevin leans back in his chair and watches his mom throw her hands up into the air, eagerly gesturing as she does when she's excited. "I designed a course that mixed the sciences with the humanities, like when John Steinbeck and his friend Ed Ricketts traveled together in the Pacific."

Ann jumps in. "Ricketts wrote the in-depth catalog *Between Pacific Tides* and—"

"Steinbeck wrote *The Log from the Sea of Cortez*," Kevin finishes the sentence, catching Ann's eye.

They finish the story triumphantly together, having heard it many times. "And the two friends found that science and philosophy weren't all that different from one another, and so did we."

"All right, all right, so what, we've told this story plenty of times," Mike says.

"Only once or twice a summer—"

"Every time you teach that course again together and explain it to your students—"

"Every faculty party—" Kevin teases.

"It's a beautiful way to find each other," Morgan says.

"Thank you." Rachel throws Morgan an appreciative smile and then rolls her eyes at her children and turns to kiss her husband on the mouth with exaggerated aplomb.

"Gross," Kevin and Ann say together as their dad returns the kiss with equal fervor. It's an old joke in the Luong household; both Kevin and Ann are used to it by now. Mike Luong and Rachel Jenners were both innovative researchers in their fields, darlings in their respective departments of marine biology and English at Cal State San Luis Obispo. Kevin was too young to remember the excitement when they got married, but he's grown up with the stories and seen how other professors treat his parents with pride and admiration for their happy marriage as well as their research and joint teaching.

Morgan doesn't seem to find Kevin's parents' affection off-putting at all. He watches them, eating his food happily.

"Well, I'm glad you're here," Rachel says. She winks at Kevin, making him blush, but at least she isn't referring to Morgan as his boyfriend.

"I'm happy to be here," Morgan says, and then makes plans with Kevin to go surfing tomorrow.

Maybe summer isn't going to be so lonely after all.

* * *

"YOU DON'T HAVE a surfboard?" Kevin asks, holding up his own longboard and walking up to the lifeguard tower where he agreed to meet Morgan.

Morgan shakes his head. He's wearing the same shorts, the ones he wore yesterday and the day before. Kevin notices now that they were in the heap of lost and found clothes Sally gave him the first day he saw Morgan.

"Okay, so you're body surfing then? Where's your wetsuit? I remember you had one."

"Safe," Morgan says. For a second Kevin thinks he sees a flash of worry cross his face, but it's soon replaced by an excited, eager expression.

Kevin tugs the cord at the back of his own wetsuit, pulling up his zipper. It's chilly, and he's sure the water will be even colder. He guesses Morgan is trying to build up a tolerance, but figures if they only swim an hour or two it'll be all right.

They dash into the water, and Kevin shivers. He ducks his head under to adjust more quickly and resurfaces to find Morgan swimming ahead.

All the clumsiness Morgan showed on the hike—walking with an unsteady gait, tripping over his feet—all of it seems to disappear. Kevin is astonished to see his new friend joyfully dive headfirst into an oncoming wave with his body undulating gracefully in the sparkling water.

Kevin tries his best to keep up, paddling fiercely on his board, blinking salt water out of his eyes. A wave swells and raises him up, heading for shore. They're not quite at that sweet spot yet, but Kevin is already tired just watching Morgan swim carelessly about in small circles, heading forward and then coming back behind Kevin.

He finally gets a chance to rest when they get to a nice spot where bigger swells are visible from a distance and the small waves nudge by. Kevin bobs in the water, catching his breath, with Morgan treading water next to him.

"You okay?" Kevin asks, then immediately realizes his question is useless. It's clear from the contented look on Morgan's face how relaxed he is. "Do you wanna hang onto my board or something?"

"I do not need to rest, thank you," Morgan says, laughing brightly. Water drops cling to his eyelashes, catching the morning sun, framing his golden brown eyes. Morgan blinks, and the gleaming drops trickle down his cheeks. He flicks his head back so water runs down his throat in rivulets. "Does that look acceptable?" he asks, pointing at an oncoming swell.

"Awesome." Kevin turns around and paddles fiercely, hoping he can catch the wave. He's not the best surfer, despite his love for the ocean and the sport. He's a fair swimmer, but doesn't have the self-discipline to practice surfing on his own, and he's never had anyone interested in going with him. So, he's never actually stood up and ridden a wave all the way to shore.

The water rises beneath him, and Kevin grips the edges of the board and tries to get to his feet. The wave rushes by and then churns over on itself. Kevin loses his balance and topples off the board. It's a mad, whirling rush of confusion underwater, and he can feel himself getting pulled quickly toward shore by the leash on his board.

Everything is green and blue and Kevin can't make out which way is up, can barely see his own hands in front of him, can't concentrate through the roar of water in his ears. If he doesn't right himself soon, he's going to get a full body drag onto the grainy beach, and it's going to *hurt*.

He feels a brushing touch at his ankle and then the leash is off, and Kevin is hauled up to the air. He gasps for breath, coughing and spluttering. Morgan is holding him up. They tread water together; Morgan watches him with a worried expression and keeps his hand clasped firmly around Kevin's arm.

"Thanks, dude," Kevin says. "I guess we're even now." He chuckles.

Morgan doesn't laugh, just blinks and asks, "Were we odd?"

"I saved you, you saved me, even-steven. You know, fair and square." Kevin gestures between them. Not for the first time he wonders where Morgan is from. Maybe he was home-schooled; his English seems centuries old sometimes. "Oh no, my board!" he shouts, swimming quickly toward the beach. Kevin's feet drag against the pull of the incoming waves. His board has drifted off to a pile of sharp rocks; the surf pummels it relentlessly.

Kevin pulls it off the rocks, groaning when he sees scratches and a huge gouge running down the center, exposing the foam interior.

Morgan clambers onto one of the rocks and eyes the board. "It is damaged?"

"Yeah. I mean, technically I could take it back out and keep going, but then the seawater will get in this crack and it'll just get worse."

Kevin walks over to the shower area, sprays down his board and rinses it carefully to get all the saltwater off. "Guess no more surfing for today."

"We could watch a movie," Morgan suggests.

"Yeah, that sounds good. Do you wanna go home and change out of your wet clothes?" The question is already out of his mouth before Kevin remembers he has never asked if Morgan lives in town, or if he moved recently to the area or to Piedras Blancas itself. He must live close by, walking distance probably; he always seems to just show up at Kevin's house. It's possible he's staying in San Simeon or farther south in Cambria. Kevin can't remember anyone dropping him off, but that doesn't mean someone hasn't.

Morgan shakes his head.

"What, you got dropped off and now you're stuck till you get picked up?" Kevin asks. "How long did you think we'd be out?"

Morgan gives him a noncommittal shrug.

"Okay, you can borrow something from me."

Should he mention that Morgan still has his sweatshirt? *He wasn't wearing it yesterday or today; maybe he thought it was a gift?* For some reason that doesn't bother Kevin at all. Morgan looked adorable wearing his blue sweatshirt. *Does Morgan have it in his room? Did he keep it because it reminded him of me?*

They walk back to Kevin's house, and Kevin laughs at Morgan's imitation of a seagull. Morgan sticks out his tongue. "Pests."

"So true," Kevin says, laughing. "You should see the school around lunchtime. Right before the bell rings, they all swarm in, waiting to attack the trashcans and the food left out. They can get quite vicious."

Morgan laughs, squawking ridiculously and flapping his hands, making a silly face.

"Are you staying in Piedras Blancas?" Kevin asks.

Morgan shakes his head. "A bit farther north. My family is only staying here for the summer."

"Oh." Kevin is more than a little disappointed that Morgan won't be going to high school with him in the fall. He'll be gone come September, back to Scotland or something.

"Come on." Kevin takes Morgan's hand, suddenly filled with the desire to make more of his time with this strange and compelling boy.

They wander into the house, wipe their wet feet on the welcome mat, climb up the stairs and giggle as they pass Ann's bedroom. She's dancing with her headphones on, oblivious to the open door, swaying to the beat.

In Kevin's bedroom, he quickly scrounges up some clean shirts and shorts. "Here, you can wear this," he says, handing an outfit to Morgan and then ducking into his bathroom to change. He peels off the wetsuit and hangs it up in his shower, then leans his surfboard carefully against the wall, eyeing the crack. He'll have to fix it tomorrow.

When he returns, Morgan is holding onto the wet boardshorts, wearing the outfit Kevin gave him. He looks curiously at the rock collection prominently displayed on Kevin's bookshelf. "These are beautiful," he says.

"Here, I'll take that," Kevin says, holding out his hand for the bedraggled boardshorts to hang in his shower. He's certain now that they're the ones from the lifeguard's lost and found. Kevin's starting to worry that Morgan doesn't have any other clothes, but he doesn't know how to bring it up. Money can be a touchy subject.

Morgan holds Kevin's favorite specimen, a piece of green olivine on basalt. Kevin once almost convinced Ann it was an avocado roll—it certainly looks like one, bright green speckled with sesame seeds, wrapped in dark seaweed.

"That's from Mexico. My family went on vacation to Baja last year, and I got that out of an old volcano." He tries his best to describe the sweltering heat and the excitement of finding geodes and cracking them open with a hammer. Morgan listens in rapt silence as Kevin talks about the find and tilts the olivine so it catches the light. He sets it back in its spot behind its label, slowly so as not to disturb the other specimens, and Kevin is quietly pleased with Morgan's careful appreciation.

"I changed my mind," Kevin blurts out.

"About what?"

"I do want this to be a date. For us, to do that," he says, blushing. "I like you. A lot."

Morgan's face breaks into a bright, happy smile.

"And what do we do differently, for this to be a date?"

Kevin can feel the heat on his cheeks. "We can hold hands, if you like. Um, or kiss, if you want to. But we don't have to do anything you don't want to. I'm fine just hanging out and watching a movie with you."

Morgan tilts his head and steps closer. "I want to," he says, not specifying what, but Kevin knows immediately.

It's just the quickest brush of lips, but Kevin feels it all the way to his toes. A warm curl of excitement blooms throughout his body, and Morgan's mouth is warm and wet against his. It's not like any kiss he's had, chaste and sweet and over in a second, and yet his heart is still pounding after Morgan leans back. He's close enough for Kevin to be able to count the eyelashes dark against his cheek.

Morgan ducks his head and asks, "Was that okay?"

"Yeah. Yeah, that was great."

They settle down on the floor, leaning back against his bed. Kevin drags his laptop across the carpet from where it was sitting in the corner and pulls up the Netflix account he shares with his sister.

"Okay, so, movies," he says distractedly as Morgan's fingers brush against the back of his hand. "What do you want to watch?"

"Whatever you like. I enjoy stories of all kinds."

Kevin finally decides on an old Batman movie, slings a casual arm around Morgan's shoulders and hits "play." The movie is an old favorite of Kevin's, and it's actually more entertaining to watch Morgan's eyes widen and the little shakes he makes when he gasps with surprise and his quiet fascination with the Penguin.

Morgan relaxes into his arm, leaning into the touch; his head rests on Kevin's shoulder. It's pleasant and comfortable in a way Kevin's never felt. He's completely at ease.

SIX.

MORGAN HATES TO admit to Naida when she's right, but movies are absolutely fascinating. It's only been a week but Kevin's shown him many different stories. He always loved stories as a child, curled up as a pup, sleepily listening as his aunts and uncles wove magical tales with their words. Sometimes they were histories of their people, sometimes clever fantasies of heroes and monsters of the ocean's depths, epic tales that took weeks to finish telling.

Movies are *visual.*

Clearly Kevin is used to it, but the first story he showed Morgan—the tale of a Batman, fighting for justice against the Penguin, the colorful costumes, the exciting music, the way the whole story came together—was so thrilling. It makes Morgan wonder if any of the penguins he's met down south could also be shape-shifters.

Morgan had been afraid Kevin would make fun of his very obvious first time enjoying a movie, but Kevin seemed happy just to watch it with him, holding him close.

And the movies weren't even the best part: Kevin said *he wanted it to be a date.*

Morgan sighs happily, drifting in the water, watching the sunlight bounce off the waves, listening to the quiet burble of fish swimming under him, feeling the water cool under his back. He swims lazily, thinking about the way they kissed, about Kevin's lips soft and sweet on his own, about Kevin's arm around him as they watched the movie.

He's lightheaded even now, thinking about it. Morgan doesn't notice when a wave pulls him forward, just lets it carry him wherever.

Morgan can't believe he's avoided the human form his whole life. Running, walking, eating fried foods—it's all amazing. Holding hands and kissing—that's a whole other experience Morgan can't believe. He's seen the affectionate nuzzling of mated pairs in his herd, the easy way they sprawl over each other when they sleep. And occasionally, when he was younger and curious, couples mating, rutting together on the beach, making loud passionate noises into the night.

It's different with humans. He doesn't know if Kevin wants to mate with him or not. He hasn't Requested that, not that Morgan can remember anyone ever in history Requesting someone to mate with and the Sea actually granting it. Requests are granted based on purity of heart, to those whose intentions are good. Kevin wanted someone to love—and Morgan does love him.

Morgan's pretty sure he could figure it out—mating—if Kevin wanted to. He's happy where they are, though, and more than thrilled about kissing. The human body—the skin—isn't as sensitive as a seal's, but the lips are particularly receptive to touch Morgan learned.

And Kevin is a patient teacher. The first time Kevin's tongue touched his own, Morgan's face turned so red he thought he must have been ill. Kevin laughed, called him adorable, and then Morgan discovered that feeling excessively warm in the face was not the sudden onset of human disease, but *blushing*.

It happens around Kevin a lot, particularly when they kiss, but Morgan loves every moment—Kevin's soft hands holding his own, or gently cupping his jaw, the warmth of his mouth, his pleased hum when Morgan tilts his head and kisses back eagerly.

It isn't always kissing and holding hands. They spend time doing other things, such as studying for the SAT together. Kevin assumes Morgan needs to study for this too, so they do it together, memorizing definitions and practicing math problems. Morgan's rather abysmal at the math, and returns to the Sea at night to try to fill in the missing gaps in his knowledge. Asking to absorb the information simply results in an amused feeling and silence, and nothing changes when Morgan tries to explain that being good at math is necessary to fulfill Kevin's Request. The Sea is silent and entertained. No one else in the herd experienced in human knowledge is any help either.

Kevin doesn't find his lack of mathematical knowledge weird. They have the same level of understanding of most of the concepts, and being bad at math is a normal human thing. Morgan does all right with the meanings and stories part, and he is learning a lot, but mostly he feels good about helping Kevin study.

One warm afternoon, Morgan accidentally knocks over a pack of index cards, sending them flying off the bed. Kevin laughs and the two of them scramble over the floor, picking up the cards together, chuckling as they bump heads. Morgan reaches for the cards scattered under Kevin's bed, crawling under it to collect them all. He shifts aside a few objects, pulling them out so he can grab all the blank cards where they're sticking to the carpet. Morgan gathers all the cards and emerges, knocking aside a box he moved earlier, grinning triumphantly at Kevin.

"Here you go." Morgan hands the cards to Kevin, who's turned a bright red.

"Uh, thanks." Kevin ignores Morgan's outstretched hand and tries to stuff a number of colorful objects back into the upended box.

"What's all this?" Morgan sets the cards down and watches.

"Nothing! It's nothing." Kevin shoves the box back under the bed, picking nervously at his shirt. His cheeks are flushed, and Morgan can smell Kevin's embarrassment.

There's a bright blue square package that Kevin missed, and Morgan picks it up curiously. The label reads *Cal State San Luis Obispo Student Health Services.* Is it some sort of medical product?

"Ah, yeah, that's uh, I don't have that because I was planning to, um, I mean, if you—I mean I already had those!" Kevin stammers. "When I came out to my parents, they were, like, super supportive, and my mom got all this stuff for me from her work."

"Are you ill? This is some sort of health product?"

"That's a condom, Morgan. Have you… never seen one before?" Kevin blinks at him.

Morgan shakes his head.

"You can open it and look at it if you want. I know not everyone has access to, like, proper sex education, or very enthusiastic parents like mine."

Morgan raises his eyebrows when he hears the word "sex" and tears open the package to look at the object inside. It's a soft ring of manmade material, slightly wet to the touch. It smells… kind of sweet. He brings it up to his nose, and the fruity scent gets stronger, and Morgan sticks his tongue out to taste it.

"Oh my God, stop," Kevin says, almost hysterically. "You're ridiculous—what are you doing?"

Morgan unravels the thing to reveal a floppy tube, sniffing at it to see if the scent persists. "Why does it smell like the candy you had me try yesterday?"

Kevin looks at the package. "Uh, I guess this one is blueberry flavored."

Morgan doesn't know what blueberries taste like, so he licks the condom, making a face at the sharp tang of the material and the too-sweet stickiness. Kevin starts laughing, and the embarrassed tension in the air gives way to fond amusement.

"You haven't explained what this is," Morgan says.

"I did!" Kevin blurts out. He buries his face in his hands. "It's for sex," he adds in a stilted whisper.

Morgan stops himself before making a comment about humans and their strange mating practices that require these extra things. Maybe these fruity-flavored things are like a courting gift that you present to your intended. But Kevin said it was for sex. Morgan gives him a blank look. "How?"

"Wow, you are really sheltered." The scent of embarrassment is back in the air. Kevin gestures hopelessly and looks at Morgan, but the human gesture is completely lost on him. "You know…."

Morgan shakes his head and scoots closer.

Kevin toys with the hem of his shirt. "Um, it's like, for protection. You put it on your penis. There are different kinds for people with different genitals; I think my mom may have gotten just a bunch of stuff." He takes the box out now and starts rifling through it, and Morgan peers closer. In addition to the small foil squares, there are different colorful packages in different sizes and a number of bright, glossy pamphlets.

Morgan unfolds one to a diagram. "*Proper Preparation and You*," he reads aloud. The illustration looks like nothing he's ever seen before, and he says as much to Kevin. "What is this?"

"I think… that's a butt."

"A butt?" Morgan shrieks. It isn't long before Kevin is laughing with him, and the two of them dissolve into unrepentant giggling. They go through the rest of the contents of the box, looking through and reading some of the pamphlets. It's fun, especially when Kevin starts reading aloud from some of the pamphlets in an exaggerated voice, as if he's performing a part in a story.

"This is kind of cool," Kevin says, when they're putting the box back under the bed.

"What is?"

"How you're not, like, embarrassed about any of this. It's just interesting to you, like we might as well be learning about world history or something." Kevin looks at him with an appreciative smile.

Morgan shrugs. "It *is* interesting, the mechanics of sex. It's nothing to be embarrassed about."

Kevin looks at him expectantly, pushing himself off the floor. He stands there with an air of nervousness, as if he's waiting for Morgan to say something else about the sex supplies, but Morgan just takes Kevin's offered hand and smiles. "Thank you for sharing this with me. It was fun."

"Yeah, it was." Kevin seems surprised but pleased. He hugs Morgan and kisses him quickly on the cheek, relaxing into Morgan's arms. "Do you wanna stay for dinner?"

"Thank you, but I'm expected at home." Technically Morgan is allowed to spend as much time as he wants on land for his Request, but he knows it would be strange if he were around all the time, and he's been trying to keep up the appearance of being human.

Kevin walks him to the door and kisses him softly. "Are you free tomorrow?"

Morgan nods.

Kevin beams at him; the smile stretches across his face from ear to ear. "Great! See you then."

"I love you! Goodbye!" Morgan hugs him once more, and Kevin pats him stiffly on the back.

"I—okay—goodbye," Kevin stammers, waving as Morgan walks away from the house.

It's high tide when Morgan gets back to the beach, but that's no problem for him, even in his human form. He dives headfirst into the waves, heading sidelong for the hidden cave where he's stashed his pelt. The salty air is cold and crisp on his wet skin, and he shivers a little as he surfaces for air. Taking a deep breath, Morgan finds the cave floor and tugs his pelt free of the rock trapping it on the ground. He takes care to fold up Kevin's sweatshirt neatly and secure it with the rock, then stuffs the shorts haphazardly next to it.

Transforming takes only a moment, for Morgan to think about his seal form and call it forward. With the next wave, Morgan is a seal again, sleek and powerful, heading toward the horizon. Despite the late hour, the sun still hangs above the water, gleaming yellow and making the waves sparkle and dance. Morgan hears the cries of seagulls in the air and the distant barks of the seals sunning themselves on the beach.

Morgan barks a greeting to them as he swims past, and the response is convoluted, a rush of noise and laughter, the sense of *warmhappyfedwarmhappyfed*. There's good hunting near here, Morgan surmises from the way one of them in the water is barking at him, but he can't understand properly what she's saying.

She gestures to him, as if she wants him to follow, and Morgan tries to tell her he's on his way home to his own herd, and to convey his thanks, but he knows she probably doesn't understand his words. She yips out a reply, and swims back to join her own herd at the rookery.

Morgan shakes his head and continues the long swim back home. Selkies and their more mundane cousins have always been able to communicate, and it's never bothered him before that it's not exact… they're just different. But this seal reminds him of one he met before on his travels, a seal that was part of another selkie herd, up in the icy waters. The selkies treated her like family, hunting with the seal and talking with her. He wondered at the time how the seal had come to be with them, but he quickly put it out of his mind in favor of following his sister and their new friends in a game of ice sliding. Morgan remembers it now in startling clarity, thinks about his "conversation" with that other seal, and how he might feel if she were his sister.

He takes a deep breath of air and dives. It's better to focus on Kevin, how their relationship is faring, and whether the Request is going well. The Sea churns around him with nothing but approval and more information about humans, if he wants it right now.

Morgan does not. He wants to understand why it makes Kevin uncomfortable when Morgan tells him he loves him. He wants to know what he's doing wrong.

He gets to the beach shortly after sunset, as the glowing pink sky is fading to purple. Naida is singing a story, acting out the humorous verses about a selkie from the warm waters who loved a selkie from the icy north. The song is silly and the pups are laughing, rolling around on the sand. Linneth watches her daughter with a doting smile, swaying with the rest of the herd, caught up in the light mood of the song.

Morgan shuffles to the circle and watches from a few feet away, not wanting his conflicting emotions to bring down the atmosphere. Linneth catches his eye and whispers something softly to the selkie next to her. In a flash she's transformed, tall and stately, draping her pelt around her shoulders and walking gracefully over to Morgan on her human legs.

"Hello, Mother."

"Morgan." Linneth kisses him on the head. "Why don't you take a walk with me?"

"Sure."

Morgan is still tired from his swim, so he's a little off balance when in human form again. His mother catches him gently by the elbow and guides him up the shore, away from the others.

"How are you? I know that every night you've returned with many stories of you and Kevin, and how wonderfully you're getting on, but you have that look."

"What look?" Morgan sighs.

Linneth smiles at him and sits on a boulder, then pats the space next to her. She doesn't say anything, just looks up at the stars. They're starting to come out, glimmering at them from millions of miles away.

Morgan watches the sky with his mother, staring at the infinite silence above them, puzzling over what he wants to ask and how to say it. A wave gently comes ashore, trickling over their feet, bringing with it the slight touch of the Sea. Morgan supposes he could always ask the Sea, but he doesn't know what kind of answer he would get, and how much of it would be something he already knows, and how he would have to struggle to figure out what it meant.

"The humans often look to the sky for answers," Linneth says, so softly it's almost to herself. The starlight reflects in her eyes as she gazes skyward.

"And are they there?" Morgan blinks at the stars.

Linneth shrugs. "Perhaps. It's an inspiration to them, but in my experience, a person may find the answer they seek simply in laying out their problem."

Morgan stares at his feet, at the imprint they make in the sand, watching the water trickle slowly back down to the ocean.

"Or you can always ask me." Linneth's laughter tinkles like bells.

"Is—is love different for humans and selkies?"

His mother does not answer, and Morgan looks over to see her lost in thought. "I don't believe so," she finally says. "Why do you ask?"

"I love Kevin, but every time I tell him, he gets—I don't know how to describe it. Like he just doesn't know how to respond and he's really uncomfortable." Morgan wiggles his toes into the sand.

After a long silence with nothing but the stars blinking at them, his mother speaks. "You ask if love is different for humans and selkies, and at the core of it, I do not think it means different things to us. But that's not what you're asking, is it, Morgan? You want to know why your overtures are received differently."

"I'm just telling him how I feel!"

Linneth smiles at him and runs a hand through his hair. "How do you know you love him?"

"I read his heart the first time I saw him."

"The humans do not share this gift of ours. How do you think they love?"

Morgan falters, thinking about the body he's in, how limited life must be for them. He takes a deep breath, feeling the grains of wet sand sticking between his toes, and thinks about how humans must love one another, the movies he's seen, the way Kevin's parents look at each other. It's like one of those math problems he has trouble understanding, as if it's in a different language. Which is silly, since he can understand all the human languages, but he can't quite answer this question.

His mother gives him a small smile and taps him under the chin. "It is the selkie way to be able to see inside someone's heart, the way we have been able to throughout all our history. To know each other instantly gives us the chance to recognize compatible partners in our brief encounters with other herds, so we might have the most information available to decide whether to leave with another herd or not."

Morgan nods. This is not new to him, but he has to wonder how humans pick their mates.

His mother laughs lightly at his confused face and explains. "Humans take time to look for mates, getting to know them over the course of their lives. Surely you've noticed that in your time with Kevin you've learned more about him than what you saw in your initial reading."

Morgan nods.

"There's a difference between falling in love and just knowing you love him," Linneth says. "And I'm happy that you have this opportunity to do both. The human way is quite rewarding, you know."

Thinking about this answer, Morgan leans into his mother's side. She draws her arm around his shoulders and strokes his skin in soothing circles. Morgan thinks he understands; he likes the idea of this—falling in love the human way, slowly, the way Kevin would. If he feels that way.

"What if—"

Linneth shushes him and points toward the sky.

"I am sure he adores you," she says after a long moment of nothing but the sound of the waves and their soft breaths. "He brings you food gifts and takes you to see beautiful things and shares stories with you. Everything you have told me about him only assures me that your choice to take this Request was the right one, that this will be a good experience for you."

"The Council chose me."

"You chose Kevin. You heard his Request first, made contact with him and, even if you did not know it at the time, you chose to be that person he needed. I understand, Morgan. I know that I am old and your mother, but I have loved before, you know."

"I know." Morgan rolls his eyes. He doesn't remember his mother's old mate, Erik, the father of Naida and his other older siblings, but everyone in the herd always talked about what a wonderful pair they made, how kind and loving he was, before his untimely death at the jaws of a shark. And Morgan knows his mother is happy with Joren, her current mate. He grew up with fond memories of Joren, and learned to hunt thanks to his calm and steadfast teaching manner. He doesn't know why his mother needs to remind him of this, that she's loved before. He has plenty of siblings to remind him of that fact.

"I'm talking about your father, Morgan."

Morgan turns to look at her.

"Don't look so shocked. I'm just surprised you never ask me about him, that's all."

"I have!"

"Not since you were a pup," Linneth chides.

"I didn't want to bring up sad memories. I used to wonder if, looking at me, you would see—him."

"Sometimes, maybe, in the curve of your jaw or the way that you laugh. It doesn't make me love you any less, you know. You are your own person, Morgan, not just my son or your father's son." Linneth kicks at the water, playfully splashing Morgan.

"What was he like?"

Linneth's smile turns melancholy, and Morgan regrets the question now, even though she was the one to bring up his father. "Now *that* would be bringing up sad memories," she says softly. "Do not worry about your Kevin feeling strange when you announce your affections; it doesn't mean he isn't enjoying your company. You are doing a wonderful job."

"Thank you, mother."

She stands up. "Do you have any other questions I can answer right now?"

Morgan shakes his head.

"I'm going to spend some time with the Sea. You enjoy the rest of your night, darling." Linneth kisses Morgan softly on the forehead and walks into the surf. She transforms easily and dives into the ocean.

Morgan watches her resurface and float on her back. The moonlight glitters on the water, and his mother is a lone shadow looking toward the silhouetted land in the distance.

* * *

AS NATURAL AS it seems to tell Kevin how he feels, in the days that follow Morgan swallows back the "I love you" he wants to say. It still comes out sometimes, but he's doing a lot better, or maybe Kevin's getting used to it, because Kevin just smiles and accepts his affection, though he doesn't say anything in return.

One afternoon Morgan is sprawled across Kevin's bed with his head in Kevin's lap as he holds up flashcards for Kevin; he smells Kevin's contentment as he combs his fingers through Morgan's hair. He is about to comment on that scent, but then remembers what Naida had told him: Some of his selkie senses will carry over to his human form, including a distinct sense of smell, his swimming abilities and seeing in the dark. He must be careful of mentioning them, as humans find them strange.

Being a selkie is not always an advantage. Unused to legs instead of flippers, at first Morgan huffs and puffs behind Kevin when they hike. He gets much better, though, and now feels as secure walking on two legs as he does swimming. He's even confident walking along the shifting docks as they bob with the waves in the harbor, while holding hands with Kevin as he points out the boathouses.

They hike all over San Simeon State Park, and soon each and every trail is familiar to Morgan. From the way he eagerly shows Morgan his favorite viewpoints or pulls him over to look at his favorite informative signs, it's clear that Kevin's spent a lot of time here.

A sign about seals overlooking a view of the ocean is one of Kevin's favorites. It makes Morgan laugh. The first time they saw it, Kevin clapped his arms to his sides and wobbled around, trying to imitate a seal.

"That's not how we—they walk," Morgan said.

Kevin didn't seem to notice his slip-up, just laughed and made a sharp barking sound. He did his best seal impression, clapping his arms together as if they were flippers, and Morgan threw his head back and laughed at the sight. "You're ridiculous."

"They're so cute and chubby." Kevin gestured at the illustration. "Not as cute as you, though," he added, touching Morgan's soft cheek and then kissing him soundly on the lips. Morgan kissed back delightedly. Kevin's lips were soft and warm, and Morgan just learned a clever thing to do with his tongue that would coax a happy little noise from Kevin. It was perfect, right there on the bluffs, with the wind blowing in their hair, the cool, crisp sea air and the view of the ocean stretching out for miles.

At least until they were interrupted by a gruff voice. "You're blocking the sign, you two."

Morgan and Kevin sprang apart and backed away. The owner of the voice was a grimy man with unkempt hair, wearing clothes splattered with fish scales and flecks of grease. His skin was dry and chapped, cheeks pink from many years in the sun. He might have been handsome once, despite the wild gray-peppered beard, but he had the look of a man who had stopped caring about his appearance long ago. "Seals," the man muttered, stepping up to the exhibit sign and scowling at it. He spat at the ground.

"You're Jenners' and Luong's kid, aren't you?" the man asked, jerking his head at Kevin.

"Yes," Kevin said, narrowing his eyes and stepping in front of Morgan.

"Who's this, then? Never seen you round these parts before a few weeks ago. Not a tourist, either. You've been here too long for that."

"I'm Morgan." He offered his hand for the man to shake, because that was what he'd learned humans did when they met. The man only stared at him unflinchingly, frowning at Morgan's face as if it offended him somehow.

"My boyfriend," Kevin announced, taking Morgan's hand and squeezing it. "He's visiting for the summer."

"Summer love, eh." The man kicked a loose rock over the edge of the cliff. It bounced down the bluff to hit the water far below. "I loved someone, once. They always leave you in the end."

"C'mon, let's go," Kevin whispered. He tugged Morgan's hand, and they backed away from the stranger.

Touched by the man's apparent sadness, Morgan wanted to hear more, but Kevin's lips were pressed in a thin line, and he'd rolled his eyes at the story.

"Don't worry about him," Kevin whispered. "He's just Old Man Floyd. Apparently he used to be a really good fisherman, but then his wife left or something and now he's drunk all the time and tells sad stories to anyone who will listen."

Kevin's voice must have carried, because Floyd turned abruptly. "She didn't leave!" Floyd said, eyes glittering. "She was stolen from me! Stolen by the Sea!"

Something about the way he said it made Morgan pause. Surely the heartbroken fisherman meant the sea, the way humans referred in general to their ocean as the mundane, passive thing they thought it was, not the terrible and beautiful Sea filled with magic and mystery.

Morgan quickly forgot about the man and his ranting, though, since he was distracted by Kevin's smile, his soft, brown eyes and the way Kevin ran ahead along the trail and let Morgan chase him. Morgan thought it was a game similar to one he had played as a child with his siblings and cousins, and ran into Kevin, head butting him. It didn't work out as well on land as it did in water, and they both tumbled to the ground.

Kevin laughed, though, with dirt smudged on his cheek, and then he kissed Morgan again. He tasted of iron and salt.

There's much of the park to explore, and one memorable afternoon Kevin took him to a bridge near the Washburn campground, a rickety old wooden walkway that cut through the trees above an expanse of green. They held hands as they walked along the path and stopped on the bridge to watch the wind flutter through the leaves. It was soft and quiet there, and Morgan wanted to tell Kevin about swimming through kelp forests, watching the sunlight filter through the tall stalks of seaweed. There was a lot he wanted to tell him, but Morgan settled for enjoying the moment.

And there are a lot of moments.

With Naida's help, Morgan figures out a reasonable schedule for someone living "a bit north" of Piedras Blancas, who might get dropped off in town to spend time with his boyfriend. Naida even helps him invent a story about his "human" family and not having enough money for him to have his own cell phone. When Kevin asks for his number, Morgan has this explanation ready, but doesn't get further than saying he doesn't have one; Kevin just nods and moves past the subject.

Morgan doesn't come to Kevin's house every day. He spends his nights swimming back to his family's beach, then telling anyone and everyone who will listen about his and Kevin's adventures, how amazing it all is. He sleeps in a close pile of his brothers and sisters, and wakes at dawn to swim back to Piedras Blancas. He stashes his sealskin in the cave, then walks to Kevin's house.

They usually go for a hike in the morning, either up on the cliffs or down by the shore, and then eat lunch, something Kevin puts together in his home. Morgan feels a little guilty about eating so much of his food, but when he offered to bring Kevin another food gift, Kevin laughed and said, "That fish you brought last time was amazing, but I don't think my mom will let my dad deep fry anything else for months. Don't worry about it."

Apparently that also meant Kevin noticing when Morgan discovered sour cream and onion-flavored potato chips. The salty greasy chips are his favorite snack when he and Kevin watch movies. Morgan found five bags in Kevin's room one day and was so overcome with joy he sank to the floor, hugging all the chips to his chest.

"They're just chips," Kevin said, popping open the bag and casually offering it to Morgan.

He's not visiting Kevin today, but Morgan's thoughts are with him. He wants to do something for Kevin, give him another kind of present.

Kevin loves rocks. Morgan swims toward the shore, the beginnings of an idea pulling him forward.

He shifts, stashes his pelt in the cave as usual, pulls on the sweatshirt and shorts and makes his way to the area where Kevin and he collected rocks before.

Morgan picks up rock after rock, thinking about Kevin's collection displayed on the bookshelf in his room, and tries his best to find ones he will find interesting—sparkling colors, minerals whose names he doesn't remember, but he knows Kevin will admire. He fills the pocket of the sweatshirt with as many rocks as he can. He finds a few pieces of the green stone that Kevin liked, none as large or clear as the piece he found on their first outing, but he hopes these pieces will make him smile.

Kevin likes the strange ones, too. What if I can find him some rocks from the ocean floor—surely those will be especially interesting?

Morgan ambles back to the cave, humming happily. He places all the rocks in a secure spot next to his boulder, then reaches for his pelt.

He can't feel the soft fur behind the rock. Frowning, he tries again, feeling all around the boulder, but there's nothing but cold stone under his hands.

It's gone.

Seven.

MORGAN HASN'T SHOWN up today to hang out, and Kevin is frustrated because he doesn't have a number so he can text him to see if he's okay. Morgan shows up every other day or so, and they've hung out together so much that Kevin didn't remember he had no way to reach Morgan. Kevin's surprised how quickly the days have gone by; he's been having such a good time.

He's determined to entertain himself today, though. Something prickles at the back of his mind, and he wants to resolve a mystery. He and Morgan never found the time to hike back to the cave since that first day, and Kevin wants to know if that thing is still there.

Kevin hikes to the shore, minding his feet. The wind is strong enough to toss his hair back and forth, and the salty air nips at his cheeks. It's the beginning of low tide; he has plenty of time before the cave is flooded. He ducks into the cave, ignoring the tingling undercurrent of fear at the base of this skull, convincing himself it'll be an exciting adventure. The wind whistles sharply as it winds around the dark curves of the cavern, nudging Kevin deeper inside. The sand is cold beneath his feet, and the cave seems much more ominous now that he's by himself.

Kevin finds the boulder, but when he reaches around the back of it, he finds only the cold surface of the rock. There's still something odd about this place, with its dredged-up seaweed splayed out on the damp sand, indicating a recent tide—and a *large* piece of kelp, which should have been caught by the rocks at the front of the cave.

Kevin follows the strand of kelp to the back of the cave and notices one boulder is damper than the others, even though they all would have been touched by the tide at the same time. He feels behind this boulder and, sure enough, there it is. He pulls it out carefully, examining it in his hands. It's fur, soft and damp with seawater. It's awfully pretty, and Kevin wonders how it got there. It looks like a seal pelt with a pretty, dappled, vaguely familiar pattern of grays.

Kevin brushes the fur gently. It feels *nice* in his hands, as if he's floating on his back in the ocean with the waves lifting him up and passing him by. He wants to keep holding it. *How did it get under that rock? Why wasn't it washed away when the tide came in?*

He tucks the pelt into his backpack and gives it a reassuring pat. It's a comforting weight the entire walk home.

Kevin has something interesting to look forward to as he sits through dinner, listening idly to his parents talking about their research and his sister sulking about having to go all the way to Cambria for a movie theater. He finishes early, washes his dishes and then heads upstairs to his bedroom.

He takes the pelt out of his backpack, spreads it out on his bed, runs his hands along the speckled pattern and marvels at how soft it is. He gives it another pat before opening his laptop to research pelts. After a few minutes online, Kevin can only conclude that it can't be from any other animal. The pattern of the spots reminds him of the playful seal he met at the pier. He hopes it's not the same pelt, and that the seal from that morning is alive and happy, eating tons of fish, swimming around somewhere.

* * *

MORGAN DOESN'T SHOW up the next day, either, and Kevin's more than a little worried. Morgan's family is in the area for the summer, but he doesn't live in town; he gets dropped off somewhere in town or at the beach whenever they hang out—

Maybe Morgan's at the beach.

As Kevin walks, the possibilities get more and more intense: What if Morgan's family decided to go back home already? And he didn't even get to say goodbye? Or what if Morgan's been in a car accident or something and Kevin doesn't *know?*

It's almost dark; most of the tourists are gone. The lifeguard tower is closed, no Sally in sight. Kevin can see two girls in the distance, trying to take pictures of each other in the rapidly sinking sunset.

He spots a figure pacing frantically back and forth at the base of the pier; the orange shorts are glaringly obvious.

"Morgan!" Kevin calls out.

Morgan's head snaps up, and he's frowning. Kevin's only ever seen him in a sunny mood; it's jarring how distraught he looks with his brows furrowed and jaw tense. Kevin rushes to Morgan's side. "Hey, are you okay?"

"It's gone, it's gone, I can't find it," Morgan says, clutching his hair.

"Shh, calm down." Kevin recognizes the beginning stages of panic. He grabs Morgan's shoulders and pulls him in for a hug. Morgan's wearing Kevin's sweater again, and while part of Kevin is warm and happy about Morgan wearing his clothes the feeling is overshadowed by worry. "It's going to be okay. What's gone? Did you leave something on the beach?"

"Yeah, it's my…" Morgan starts, and then trails off, lip wobbling. Tears well up in his eyes. "I've been looking all day, and it's not anywhere—"

"Look, whatever it is, we can get you a new one." Kevin rubs Morgan's back comfortingly, holding him close. "I can help, if you don't have, um…"

Kevin sighs, presses a kiss to Morgan's forehead and tries to figure out an easy way to talk about what's obviously a money issue.

"No, this isn't something that can be replaced." Morgan wrenches himself out of Kevin's arms. He seems utterly broken and devastated, and tears stream down his cheeks. "I can't go home without it."

"All right, I'll help," Kevin says. "What does it look like?"

Morgan glances at his feet and sighs. "It's… like a seal pelt. Black and gray." His voice seems to shrink, getting smaller, as if he wants to disappear into the sand.

"Oh! I have seen one, actually. It was in that cave, near where we've collected rocks."

Morgan looks up, raising his eyebrow. "Yeah… that's mine," he says slowly.

Kevin grins, pleased to have solved the apparent problem. "Don't worry about it! I have it. It's back at my house. I didn't want it to get washed away in the tide, so I took it with me." He holds out his hand, expecting Morgan to take it so they can go back to his house and Kevin can return it to him.

Morgan goes unnaturally still.

"It's very pretty," Kevin says, not understanding the reaction. Isn't it supposed to be a good thing that Kevin found it? He's not even asking Morgan to explain why he can't go home without a seal pelt. Maybe it's very rare and valuable, and his parents would be upset if he lost it. It still doesn't make sense that Morgan was storing it in a cave, especially one that fills up with saltwater at high tide. But Kevin has had a strange feeling ever since he touched it that the sealskin is alive somehow, and wouldn't be ruined by saltwater.

Morgan stands up a little taller. "So this is it then. You want me to be yours forever?" His voice is heavy with the question.

Kevin blinks. "What? We just started dating. I didn't think we needed to talk about this right away! You're your own person, anyway; I don't think someone can belong to anyone else, no matter how much you care about them. I just wanted to give your thing back to you."

Morgan takes a deep breath and the strange, tight posture relaxes into his normal stance. "You want to give it back?"

"Absolutely."

Morgan takes his hand and squeezes it. His smile is grateful, but Kevin doesn't think he's done anything to deserve the awed look in Morgan's eyes. He squeezes Morgan's hand and kisses him softly on the cheek.

They hold hands all the way back to Kevin's house. Morgan sneaks careful glances at him the entire walk, and fondness softens his face. Morgan's always telling Kevin that he loves him, but right now it's obvious that he actually *does*. He squeezes Morgan's hand in return and is lost in his own thoughts for a while, wondering what Morgan thinks when he never says it back. Morgan knows Kevin likes him a lot, that's for sure, but love…

Kevin sneaks Morgan into the house by the back door. He doesn't want to deal with questions right now, or anyone teasing them. No one notices them tiptoe upstairs—Ann is too engrossed by the television and his parents are discussing something excitedly; the whiteboard has been wheeled into the living room and has various formulae scribbled on it and several technical books are open and scattered across the dining table.

Kevin shuts his door carefully. He pushes past his clothes to the back of his closet and takes out the pelt.

"Here you go." Kevin hands it to Morgan, who takes the pelt with a reverent, breathy gasp. "Did you say it's *like* a seal pelt?" he asks carefully, remembering what Morgan said on the beach.

Morgan clutches the pelt to his chest. He stands lightly on the balls of his feet with a bright, luminous smile on his face. "I can show you. Come on."

Kevin groans. They just snuck in, and now they're sneaking out again? He was hoping to ask if Morgan might want to cuddle and make out for a while, maybe even stay over, fall asleep together.

Kevin grabs Morgan's arm. "Hold on, don't go stomping out there unless you want my parents throwing condoms at us and making the most awkward jokes. What are you showing me? I've got my laptop and the entirety of the Internet right here. I think you could find anything you wanted to show me, you know, in the comfort of my room. Where we are, together. And no one knows you're here yet, so." He waggles his eyebrows hopefully at Morgan.

"It's not on your Inner Net." Morgan shakes his head. "I really want to share this with you, Kevin." Something about the way he's holding himself, standing in Kevin's bedroom self-consciously, sincere brown eyes looking up hopefully him, makes Kevin's stomach flutter.

"All right, let's go." Warmth blooms inside him when he sees Morgan smile from ear to ear.

They creep out slowly and quietly, and when the back door shuts Kevin sighs with relief. "Okay now, where are we going?"

"Back to the ocean!"

"Really, we just came from there," Kevin says, but follows Morgan anyway. Whatever it is, Morgan is excited about it; his pace quickens to a jog. Kevin huffs along, all the way to the beach.

The sky, caught in that nebulous time after sunset, still glows with the energy of the day, and the heavy velvet of night has yet to fall upon them. A few stars gleam through the purple twilight, as if they were too impatient to wait until dark to shine. Morgan races all the way to the water, throwing back a few looks every now and then to see if Kevin is still following him. In the distance, the silhouettes of the boats at the docks shift rhythmically with the waves. The air prickles with electricity, and the ocean seems to churn in anticipation.

Morgan shucks off the sweatshirt and shorts before Kevin can even make an embarrassed noise. He's naked now, pale and ethereal in the moonlight, and Kevin stops where he's standing with his mouth hanging open.

The shorts are kicked off carelessly, but Kevin's sweatshirt is folded delicately and placed on a dry spot on the sand.

"Morgan, what are you—?"

"Shhh, I'm showing you." Morgan turns around and presses a finger to Kevin's lips.

Kevin is definitely blushing now and he avoids looking down. "Yeah, you are." As soon as the words are out of his mouth he's aware of how cheesy he sounds. He has to laugh at himself, but he's allowed to flirt with his boyfriend, right?

Morgan gives him a mischievous look and steps toward the ocean, and Kevin is once again aware that Morgan is naked and standing unabashed in the moonlight. "Look," he says, and Kevin is unable to look anywhere else.

Morgan picks up the pelt and swings it over his shoulders, then steps forward. The incoming wave curls in on itself, creeps up the sand, then ebbs. The night is silent except for the wind, the rhythm of the waves and Morgan splashing into the ocean. The pelt seems to shrink; the space around it shimmers like air above a fire.

Another wave crashes in, and Morgan ducks right into it. Kevin cries out when he doesn't immediately reappear.

Cursing, Kevin dashes forward, ready to pull him out, but then he sees a silhouette rising out of the wave—

It's a seal.

Kevin freezes. The water rushes past his ankles and soaks through his socks and shoes, but he can't move; he's trying to figure out what just happened. Morgan is still in the water somewhere, but the seal, *the seal* came out of nowhere. If it had swum up, surely he would have noticed—

The seal barks as the waves carry him to Kevin. He falls backward, and the seal scrambles on top of him, nosing at his face in a very un-seal like manner.

Kevin looks into familiar brown eyes, and then he *knows*, even if it makes no sense.

"Morgan?"

The seal makes a happy noise and bumps a wet nose against his cheek.

"I don't really understand what's happening." Kevin pats the seal carefully on its head. There's a slight shimmering, and in the blink of an eye on top of Kevin is a naked Morgan with the pelt draped across his back like a cape. He's wet and laughing, shaking with barely contained excitement.

Morgan, all confidence and energy, kisses him. His lips are wet with saltwater, plump and full, and Kevin moans into the kiss as Morgan's tongue teases its way into his mouth. He's pressed against the shore; the wet sand sinks under their weight. The kiss is slow, euphoric, a hot contrast to the cold water ebbing and flowing around them. Morgan's body is flush against his, just the two of them and the roar of the ocean.

They break apart, gasping and grinning at each other, and Kevin can't tell if it's been five minutes or five days, he's so pleasantly disoriented.

He's not embarrassed that Morgan is naked; he's full of awe and wonder. Kevin tries to speak but all he manages is, "You're really… wow."

They sit on the beach together. The pelt is almost iridescent in the moonlight, lying across Morgan's lap. Kevin studies Morgan holding his hand, watching the way the flush on his cheeks travels down his neck and blossoms across his chest. He thinks about all the strange things Morgan has said this summer, about his reactions that made Kevin think he was just sheltered, but this— this makes more sense.

"I am a selkie," Morgan says, watching Kevin for a response. His fingers twitch nervously under Kevin's.

Kevin interlaces their fingers to show his support, and he nods, still too stunned to speak. It almost could be a dream, the velvety night all around them, softly lit by the moon and stars, Morgan sitting next to him, looking at him adoringly. Except Kevin knows the warmth of Morgan's hand is real, what he saw only a moment ago, the way his heart beats in time with the waves crashing ashore—this is all real, and his boyfriend is *magic*.

Morgan tells Kevin about his family following the current, traveling all over the world, staying in different places depending on the season; about selkies and other shape-shifters from the depths of the ocean. It's as though a whole door of possibilities has opened in Kevin's mind, casting light on every strange experience he's had, on every person who's ever mentioned "locals" no one in town has heard of.

As a seven-year-old kid, Kevin was playing in the waves, and drifted far, far from Piedras Blancas, and had no idea where he was, and another kid found him in the water, crying because he couldn't recognize the beach. The other boy just took Kevin's hand and swam with him back to Piedras Blancas, and disappeared into the waves before Kevin could invite him ashore to play. Kevin remembers being distraught that he couldn't find his new friend anywhere in town, asking everywhere for a dark-skinned boy with a gap between his teeth. Had he been a selkie? Or another shape-shifter?

"Magic. What else is there? Vampires? Werewolves?"

Morgan laughs at him. "I don't know." He smiles solemnly at him, tone changing to reverent, serious. "I can't speak for land creatures, but the Sea is deep and ancient, full of secrets."

"This explains so much about you. Why I don't see in you in other clothes, all the fish you brought—"

"I'm a good hunter." Morgan smiles, sitting a bit more upright.

"But how did you know my name? Where I lived?"

"The Sea hears many things, many stories, wishes, pleas," Morgan says quietly. "You cast seven tears at high tide, asking for a companion. We have not had a proper Request in so long that my family was bound by our code to honor it. I was put to the task."

Kevin shivers. "Wait a minute. You're only hanging out with me because of… some sad wish I made?"

Morgan shakes his head. "Kevin, I am here because I want to be."

"You just said I was a 'task,' something your people felt obligated to do because I cried my heart out into the ocean."

"A Request," Morgan corrects. "I would not have come if I had not liked what the Sea told me about you, and what I knew I loved immediately."

"I told you, you can't keep saying that, I like you a lot, but—"

"You're cold. You should remove your wet skins." Morgan tugs on the saturated T-shirt clinging to Kevin's torso. It's wet and cold and getting less comfortable by the minute, but Kevin isn't sure how he would handle it if they were *both* naked.

"It's fine," Kevin says, ignoring the growing chill. First he was thrilled to find out more about Morgan, about the supernatural, but now he's starting to wonder how much of Morgan's feelings are his own and how much is an omniscient, magical oceanic sentience showing pity on him. "I should get home. My parents know I hole myself up in my room sometimes, but it might be weird if I don't get caught creeping to the kitchen to steal snacks."

"I can walk you back to your home."

"Sure."

With the pelt carefully wrapped around his neck like a scarf, Morgan picks up Kevin's sweatshirt, dusts off the sand and then puts it back on. Kevin thinks the hood is caught on Morgan's head for a second before he realizes Morgan is pausing to breathe in the scent of it. Morgan bends over to pull on the shorts, and Kevin realizes the smattering of freckles on his bare back correlates to the spotted pattern he's seen on the seal. Kevin realizes he's staring, blushes and looks at his feet and only looks up when Morgan takes his hand again.

"You smell like anxiety," Morgan says. "Are you unhappy that I am not truly human?"

"No, it's not that." Kevin casts about for a way to explain, while he struggles to process that Morgan can *smell* his anxiety. *Has he always been able to do this?* "I just…"

"You worry that I might have been compelled to feel this way about you."

"Yeah," Kevin says in a small voice. He kicks at a stray pebble and his waterlogged shoe hangs heavily on his foot.

They stop walking, and Morgan takes both his hands and looks up at him, holding his gaze. The street is dark and empty, lit only by moonlight and a flickering streetlamp. "Kevin, when I first shifted, I wasn't quite sure how to use my human form. I'd never done it before, never wanted to, even though most of my family has had practice. You helped me, and then gave me your skin off your back. I didn't know yet that it didn't mean the same thing for humans, but I was overwhelmed by your kindness and trust."

Morgan speaks with a clear voice, confident and steady. "I chose you, chose your Request. The Council may have said they assigned me, but you had my heart long before they heard your Request and thought who best in our herd could fulfill it. I was there, I saw you, heard you, wanted to know you." Morgan lowers his gaze, looks up through his eyelashes. "The time I've spent with you has been wonderful, more than I ever could have hoped for."

"I really enjoy our time together, too. But that isn't love—we're just hanging out, you know. We're dating, having a good time. Maybe in a longer relationship after we've been through a lot of stuff, we could say we loved each other, but—"

Morgan shakes his head. "When my pelt was missing, I was terrified. I thought maybe—" He takes a deep breath; a sudden, wild fear shines in his eyes, and then the look is gone, replaced with a calm wonder. "You said you took it, but then immediately returned it to me when you found out it was mine. You didn't know what it was or what you could have done with it—you gave it back knowing only that it belonged to me and that I was unhappy."

"Yeah, it would have been a jerk move to keep it."

Morgan squeezes Kevin's hands. "Did you know my people have a history of coming ashore? We don't do it very often anymore, take human forms like this. There are stories of pelts being stolen, humans keeping us for themselves—"

"I would never do that to you."

Morgan's entire face softens. "How do you doubt that I love you?"

"It's because we're kids. We don't know what love is."

Morgan plucks a stray piece of seaweed from Kevin's hair. "It's simple. I care about you, enjoy spending time with you and want you to be happy. It's the easiest thing in the world to understand. I knew it when I saw you and you gave me the skin to wear, and I definitely knew it when you gave me back mine. It's that warm, happy feeling in your gut, you know."

He doesn't ask Kevin if he feels the same, doesn't seem to need to; seems happy to just express it, to make sure Kevin knows. There's a long-winded, complicated explanation he could give right now, but Morgan's simple definition and acceptance strikes him as an honest truth.

Maybe Kevin is the one who's making it complicated. Maybe, when he said *we don't know what love is,* he meant *I don't know what love is.* Morgan seems to have a clear idea of what love means to him and how he feels about Kevin; he has no problem being open about it. Kevin remembers Morgan's immediate declaration of feelings when they met, how he reacted with a kind of amused detachment, acknowledged Morgan's feelings but didn't feel ready or worthy of such unconditional adoration.

But he knows Morgan now, knows his inquisitive nature and his kindness, his patience and easy sense of humor, knows Morgan supports his hopes and dreams. Kevin wants to be worthy of that affection, wants to continue knowing this amazing person who's come into his life.

"Okay," Kevin says, stepping closer and pressing his face into Morgan's neck, nuzzling at the skin there. He smells like the sea, the wild surf rolling in, the sharp tang of salt, bright and clean. He kisses him quickly on the jawline, then again, peppering him with light, playful kisses until Morgan laughs, grabs his chin and kisses him soundly on the mouth.

"Come on, aren't you still cold?" Morgan teases.

"Forgot." Kevin says, a little breathlessly. The wet clothes are still heavy on him, but somehow, he's not cold at all.

EIGHT.

THAT NIGHT MORGAN takes his time swimming back to his family's beach. He knows he's later than usual—the moon is high in the sky—but he's too happy to think about it. He swims lazily, curling his body into the waves, drifting on his back to watch the moonlight and sighs happily, thinking about Kevin.

Kevin didn't run away or react with disgust when Morgan told him his secret. He only worried Morgan's feelings for him were a byproduct of fulfilling his Request, but Morgan explained it the best he knew how.

Telling him the truth was an impulsive decision, but Morgan was so overwhelmed that Kevin wanted to give him back his sealskin that he wanted Kevin to know how much that meant to him.

And even after that, Kevin made no moves to take it from him, only listened curiously as Morgan told him about what he was.

Morgan floats along carelessly, until he can feel the worried voices brushing across his skin, echoing through the water.

"We were so worried!" Naida snaps as he beaches himself. She runs into him, bumping him with her nose.

Mother is sitting by the cliffside, watching as Morgan ambles up to her.

"Sorry, I lost track of time," Morgan says.

"We were beginning to wonder if you had been stolen," Linneth says, and Morgan instantly feels guilty for making everyone worry. He cuddles up to her, feeling the solid comfort of her warmth. The sharp smell of relief is in the air, and Morgan huddles under her flipper as he did when he was a pup.

"How was your day?" Dorian asks. "Did you watch any more movies?"

The usual group huddles around them, eagerly waiting for Morgan to describe more of his adventures.

Morgan hesitates. "No, no movies today."

Dorian groans.

"What did you do?" Naida asks. "Are you mating, is that what you're doing? Humans do it differently, it requires quite a bit of preparation—"

"No, no, we're not doing that," Morgan takes a deep breath, waiting for everyone to be quiet. "I told Kevin I'm a selkie. Showed him, too." He smiles, remembering Kevin's awed look.

The rest of the selkies start mumbling, then talk over one another in short, panicked barks.

"Accidental reveals are one thing, but this is someone Morgan's been seeing for quite some time," Morgan's uncle Dinar says. "It won't be something he easily forgets."

Someone nods. "Linneth, didn't you just tell us the dangerous ones were back?"

"What? What dangerous ones?" Morgan asks.

"You haven't been around much, but I heard that this bunch badly injured one of the members of a herd that is summering on Vancouver. It was before the herd left their other home. The dangerous ones wish to capture us at any cost."

"And do what?" Morgan asks in horror.

"Study us, dissect us, whatever it is, it isn't good," Naida butts in.

Linneth waits until the talking ceases. "Do not panic," she says loudly. "I do not know if these are the same hunters who took Andav from the northern iced lands. But one of them was spotted in Piedras Blancas. The Sea has told me to be careful. I do not want anyone swimming near the Moon's Eye or south of it. If Morgan has chosen to reveal his true nature to this Kevin, it is because he trusts him. We should trust Morgan."

Morgan feels proud as her flipper rests on his back, and everyone looks at him. "As you know, Morgan is sixteen years of age now. This is his last year. It is a good experience for him, to learn the human way, and for him to have a relationship with this boy."

The rest of the seals murmur in agreement, and slowly disband, either to find a spot on the beach to sleep for the night, or to return to the incoming tide, to sleep amidst the waves.

"What do you mean, my last year?" Morgan asks, turning the words over in his head.

"Your last year as a child, of course," Linneth says. "Don't worry about it. When the summer is over, we will leave here, and you will have plenty of memories of loving this boy to warm your heart."

Something unsettles Morgan, the way his mother's eyes shift, the way she says *memories.*

When the summer is over, the Request will be fulfilled.

Morgan doesn't want to think about it.

NINE.

THEY FALL INTO a routine. Now that Kevin knows Morgan's secret, there's no more mystery about where he goes when he's not hanging out with Kevin. Morgan hides his pelt somewhere else, and he asks if Kevin wants to go with him, but Kevin refuses, even though it would be cool. He wants to show Morgan that he doesn't care where it's hidden, that he has nothing in common with those people in the stories who want to find the pelts to keep their selkie lovers human. The slow smile that spreads across Morgan's face when Kevin tells him this is completely worth giving up a little bit of his curiosity.

Morgan has his secret, and Kevin is glad of it. Neither of them brings up the subject of the pelt, and they spend their days in a happy, muddled mix of Kevin's bedroom, the state park and the ocean.

"I've always wanted to see the Moon's Eye up close," Morgan says one day while they're walking along the beach, looking for sea glass.

"The what?"

Morgan points at the lighthouse off in the distance and his ears turn red. "I wanted to ask before, but I didn't know what the human name for it was."

"The lighthouse!" Kevin grins at him. "Well, light station, technically, but no one calls it that."

They join a guided tour with a handful of tourists, and Morgan listens to the history with rapt fascination. Kevin's been here too many times to count, but it's refreshing to experience it again with Morgan.

"I like that the light helps to guide humans and their ships back to shore," Morgan says at the end of the tour. They're in the gift shop and Morgan turns over a little lighthouse model in his hands, tracing the light. "We've always called it the Moon's Eye because it shines at night, watchful, even when the moon isn't out."

"That's so cool. Do selkies have names for everything?" An elaborate world map is displayed on the wall, and Kevin brushes the familiar outline of California with his fingers, moving up the coast.

"Yes, they aren't the same as how humans name places." Morgan's hand covers Kevin's as they trace together. "California... Oregon...Vancouver... Alaska." He smiles at Kevin. "Our names have more to do with one specific location: a herd's winter home or a landmark for guiding a journey. There's an outcropping of rock here we call the Whale's Tail, and this is Kevin's Nose."

"What? Where?"

Morgan taps him on the nose. It's so quick that it takes Kevin a moment before he realizes what just happened and then bursts out in surprised laughter.

It's the best relationship Kevin's ever had. Well, technically, the only relationship. Kevin can't believe he used to count what he had with Miles as anything other than Miles using him.

That brief affair now seems like a lifetime ago: The way Kevin hung onto Miles' every word, how he was always waiting for more, rereading text messages over and over, searching for hidden meanings. Miles was only ever interested in hooking up, and Kevin was so quick to mistake that casual intimacy for actual affection. Sure, it was thrilling, making out with another person, and feeling attractive for once. But Miles ran hot and cold, eagerly touching him in the secrecy of Miles' bedroom, but ignoring him at school.

Miles wanted *more,* too. When Kevin, as a joke, showed him the supplies his parents had gotten him, Miles lit up and said, "Condoms, awesome. We can have sex now."

Kevin faltered, stumbling over his words, trying to explain that he wasn't ready—maybe when they'd been a relationship longer; after all, they'd only started figuring out how to get each other off, and he was just getting comfortable with the idea of orgasms with a partner in general.

Miles shrugged. "Whatever, just tell me when you're done waiting so we can screw."

His blunt and casual attitude took Kevin aback, and at the time he felt guilty for his own preferences, for wanting to wait. He researched the mechanics in depth, figured it would be intense and probably difficult, not something he wanted to rush into. But Miles wanted to, so Kevin decided maybe he should just go along with it. Otherwise Miles would think Kevin didn't like him as much.

Kevin is so glad Miles broke off their stupid arrangement before they had sex.

It's a good thing, because it wasn't a relationship at all.

With Morgan, Kevin has a best friend whom he can laugh with at movies, introduce to the entirety of the *Star Wars* trilogy, and a boyfriend whom he can cuddle and kiss and admire. Even studying is fun with Morgan propped up on Kevin's bed, quizzing

him on SAT words with flashcards, sticking his tongue out as he
sounds out difficult words, rewarding him with kisses when he
gets the definitions right.

Teaching Morgan things about human culture is fun, too, and
he takes to everything enthusiastically. Now that his secret is out,
Morgan has no problem asking Kevin to explain anything and
everything.

They're sprawled out on Kevin's bed, headphones split between
them, listening to Kevin's iPod. Morgan giggles as Kevin nods
his head to the music. "We do this too," Morgan says. "We have
songs that tell stories of our people, songs for fun, songs about
love." He tilts his head, bemused, listening to the song. "They're
singing incredibly fast. I can't understand what they're saying. It
is fun, though."

"Oh, I have lots of slower things. Here, listen."

Kevin takes the iPod, switches it to his "relaxing" playlist and
puts it on shuffle. The first song is Bobby Darin's "Somewhere
Beyond the Sea," and Kevin starts humming along, bumping
Morgan's shoulder playfully.

Morgan listens thoughtfully, a smile on his face, bumping Kevin
back. "This one is quite lovely," he says. "The man is hopeful,
waiting for his love so they can be together again."

"Want to listen again?"

Morgan nods, and Kevin restarts the song, watching Morgan
close his eyes as he listens, enraptured. Kevin wants to memorize
the soft curve of his cheek, that subtle smile on his face, the freckles
that dance across his nose and cheeks. It's a sweet, contented
moment, and he wants to remember exactly how it is right now:
one of Morgan's feet idly rubbing against Kevin's in a steady
rhythm, the quiet calm of the room, the pleasant jazz music
flowing through the shared headphones, the split cord swaying
as Morgan and Kevin nod their heads to the beat.

Kevin hums along with the chorus, and then Morgan surprises him when he starts to sing in a clear, buoyant voice. "We'll meet beyond the shore…" Morgan sings. His voice seems to fill the room, resonating, warm and bright, and Kevin listens, transfixed, as Morgan finishes the song. If he thought Morgan's normal speaking voice was pleasant and melodious, this is on another level. It seems almost tangible, as if Kevin can feel the hope and longing in the melody touch his skin, feel the emotions seeping into him.

Kevin is silent after the song is over, and he turns off the iPod before it can play another song. "That was beautiful," he tells Morgan.

"Thank you," Morgan says, his cheeks flushed. "I've never—I mean, I always thought I was the worst singer in the herd. My cousin Micah says it's because I'm a halfling."

Kevin furrows his brow.

"My father is human." Morgan's tone is carefully light, but he's watching Kevin, as if waiting for a reaction.

"Okay." Kevin isn't sure if this is a sensitive issue among selkies. He's reminded of the way he used to feel as a kid when his mom picked him up from school and the other students made comments about them not being the same race, asking if she was his evil stepmother, if she was going to give him mixed little brothers and sisters. Kevin knows there's nothing wrong with having a mixed heritage; if he had younger siblings he would love them just the same. "Well, I think you are an amazing singer. Your cousin sounds like an idiot."

Morgan leans closer, whispering conspiratorially, "One time before he was mated, Micah was trying to impress a selkie from another herd when we were passing by a territory much farther north. He was unaccustomed to the ice versus the sand, and when he was shuffling up to say hello to her, he completely lost his balance and fell on his face."

Kevin laughs with Morgan, imagining a smug-looking seal slipping on the ice in front of his crush.

"He's actually not that great a singer, himself," Morgan says, visibly cheered. "Everyone knows my sister Naida has the best voice in the herd."

Kevin thinks about the strange, magical way Morgan's voice seemed to touch his skin. "Hey, are all of you—when you sing, do you—is it like, magic?"

Morgan looks at him. "What do you mean?"

"Like, you know how… Okay, so humans have lots of stories of how mermaids sing, like, these magical songs to lure sailors to their deaths."

Morgan raises his eyebrows. "Yeah, well, some selkies have stories of how humans roll around in the mud all day long, but obviously that isn't true."

Kevin colors in embarrassment. "I didn't know. Well, you're obviously supernatural; I just didn't know if there were other types of… I dunno." He shrugs awkwardly, picking at the slightly pilled duvet cover. *It sucks when people ask questions based only on stories about your culture.* Miles once came for dinner, and brought his own fork out at the table and smiled at the Luongs as if he should be patted on the back for assuming they wouldn't have forks.

"Stop being so sensitive. I just wanted to make sure I could eat," Miles said during the ensuing fight. That was dumb too, that Kevin had to explain why he was mad.

Kevin takes a deep breath and lets go of the blanket. *I should have thought before I blurted out that dumb mermaid comment.* "I'm sorry," Kevin says, reaching out to Morgan.

Morgan takes his hand and strokes his thumb slowly across the back of his hand. "It is all right. I know why you would have thought so."

Morgan starts singing again, and this time it's not in any language Kevin understands. The words have a haunting lilt, echoing in the room. It's beautiful, and again Kevin can *feel* the music touching his skin, and he feels filled with sorrow in a way he can't explain.

The song finishes with a soft note that hangs in the air, and Morgan gives Kevin a sad little smile. The despondent feeling passes, and Kevin knows he doesn't need to cry, even though he can feel the tears pricking at his eyes. "What was that?" Kevin asks, his voice caught in his throat.

"That was the story of Danilae. She lived many, many years ago. She was not a selkie, but a merrow. Distant cousins of ours." He speaks slowly and evenly, as if he is used to the cadence of storytelling. "Danilae loved a human, a merchant sailor, who often sailed through the treacherous waters near the cove where she lived. They met on the cove when he could steal time away from his busy route, but it was not often. Then there was a terrible storm, one that smashed his boat to smithereens."

Kevin squeezes Morgan's hand, watching the way Morgan's face tightens with an old sorrow. Kevin's sure from the tone of the song this story isn't going to end well. Morgan squeezes back and continues with his story.

"Danilae was injured, struck by a piece of driftwood that gored her tail, and she could not swim to help him. Cast off the boat, desperately trying to swim to safety, her lover was unable to see through the storm. Danilae sang to him in hope of guiding him to shore, but it was to no avail."

Kevin's face falls. "Oh no. Did they…"

Morgan looks away. "They both died that day. I'm fairly certain this is the tale that inspired the one you know about mermaids, as you call them. The way my mother tells the story—she's quite good at it—it takes a few hours, and by the end everyone is crying." He shakes his head. "I'm certain that a number of sailors on that boat survived to tell the tale of the music they heard, and the bewitching creature that sang as their captain drowned. Tales get exaggerated as they are passed down from generation to generation. I guess I shouldn't be surprised you know of the story. Merrows are a solitary bunch; I've never met one, and, as my mother tells me, they've been hunted nearly to extinction."

"Hunted? You mean there are people who deliberately go out to—"

"Yes. I don't know how persistent it still is, but there are still zealous groups of hunters. We've always been taught to be careful of them. My older sister spent a year on land trying to locate the dangerous ones and to learn more about them, after members of other herds went missing. One selkie managed to escape, but he told a terrifying tale of a group that held him captive, attempting to study him. I think they were planning to kill him eventually, cut him open to find out how his magic worked."

Kevin curls protectively around Morgan, holding him tight. He can tell Morgan's trying to talk calmly, to convince Kevin, or himself, that this doesn't scare him at all, but Kevin can see it's more than a bit unnerving. "Hey. It'll be okay. I'm not ever going to tell anyone about you. You'll be safe."

He kisses Morgan on the forehead. Morgan closes his eyes, sighs and lets Kevin pull him close.

"Hey, I've got an idea—have you ever heard of a blanket fort?"

Morgan shakes his head, and Kevin lights up. "This is going to be great. Come on."

He gets off the bed, motioning for Morgan to join him. Kevin grabs the spare blankets from his closet and the nylon rope he has for this very purpose. Morgan is helpful, paying attention to Kevin's instructions. The rope is tied between various curtain rods and the closet door, and then blankets are thrown over it until they have a tent-like structure.

"And the final touch," Kevin says, grabbing the coil of old Christmas tree lights from his closet. He strings it along the interior of the blanket fort, then plugs it in.

Kevin holds the flap of blanket open for Morgan, gives him a little bow and says, "After you." Morgan grins, climbs inside and then gasps.

Kevin smiles proudly to himself and crawls in after Morgan. The bed has been transformed into a cozy space, illuminated by dozens of little lights, with blankets hanging around them like soft curtains. "I'm going to get my laptop and we can watch a movie or something."

Morgan grabs his hand before he can leave. "Wait." He pulls Kevin close for a kiss. It's soft and sweet, and Morgan is smiling against his lips.

It's perfect, and Kevin wants to live inside this moment forever.

Ten.

KEVIN IS EXTRA excited today when he answers the door. His mood is infectious, and Morgan immediately grins back at him. He moves to step into the house, but Kevin races past him, grabbing his hand.

"I thought you wanted to show me the saga of Mr. Indiana Jones and his three quests today," Morgan says, as Kevin pulls him outside his house and shuts his front door behind them.

"Change of plans. Ann decided last minute to go to San Francisco with her friends, and they picked her up, so the car is all mine for the entire weekend!" Kevin dangles a set of keys, which glint in the morning light.

"Okay." Morgan follows Kevin to the car. He's gotten over his initial awe at human ingenuity. It's almost the equivalent of swimming in a faster current, letting it take you farther than you can go with your own fins.

"I want to show you around! We can drive down to SLO—"

"Slow?" Morgan scrunches up his face. "I thought the last time you were telling me about cars it was about what a great driver you are, how fast you could go—"

Kevin laughs as they get into the vehicle. "No, sorry, I meant S, L, O, for San Luis Obispo. It's a much bigger city than Piedras Blancas, with lots of people and stores and buildings. I figure we've seen everything in town and San Simeon, too. Cambria is bigger, but I figure we could just go for it. Morro Bay's really pretty and we could definitely stop there, too, but you've seen lots of bays and rocks, huh?"

The car roars to life, like a beast awakening from its slumber, and Kevin taps the pink stuffed creature that hangs from the rearview mirror. "I'm sure wherever you want to take me will be excellent," Morgan says.

Kevin grins at him, takes his hand and squeezes it.

"THIS IS THE Pacific Coast Highway!" Kevin shouts joyfully into the wind. "And you know the Pacific, of course!" Kevin gestures wildly out the window at the water.

Morgan grins at the human name for this part of the ocean. It still amuses him how they separate themselves with borders and names for all their lands and waters, and he tells Kevin as much. He laughs and agrees, and says the world is a complicated, complicated thing.

They drive down the Pacific Coast Highway with the wind blowing through the open windows. From here on the cliffs, the ocean glitters, stretching blue and vast out into forever. Kevin's iPod is hooked up and the display reads: "Morgan's Playlist." Morgan leans back in the seat, wondering when Kevin collected all his favorite songs. Bobby Darin is singing as the car follows the winding road down the coast, and Morgan thinks lazily, *what a wonderful way to travel.*

Looking out the window, Morgan's home looks almost flat—a singular blue color, nothing but a surface. If he squints, he can make out specks that are surfers waiting for a wave, and in the distance a few ships. They look so small from here, so insignificant, compared to the way those monstrous vessels loom over the herd whenever they travel past.

Kevin is proud of his driving. He takes special care to let a faster car overtake them and then cut in front of them. "My dad was really particular about teaching me good driving manners."

Morgan isn't sure what the distinction between regular etiquette and driving etiquette is, but Kevin seems to be doing well operating a vehicle, so he nods.

San Luis Obispo is indeed much busier than Piedras Blancas or its neighbor to the south, San Simeon. The streets are filled with cars and shining buildings, and people walk everywhere. Kevin drives them to a crowded lot filled with even more cars of every shape and color, and he scowls in frustration, driving around and around the area, until finally he calls out in triumph and pulls the car to rest amongst all its brethren.

"What is this place?"

"Are you ready for this?" Kevin says. "This is a *mall*." He throws his arms out theatrically, and Morgan's eyes widen. They walk into the large building, which is teeming with people and color and sounds. Morgan knows what a store is; he's seen them in Piedras Blancas, and he knows the places to purchase foods are restaurants, but there are so many here, selling so many different things.

"It's a lot, isn't it?" Kevin grins at Morgan's stunned reaction. "Hey, I've been saving my allowance—I want to get you some new clothes. Come on."

Kevin leads him into a bright store filled with many adornments that the humans wear—different fabrics and colors and shapes and sizes. He goes through the racks until his arms are full of clothes, then pushes Morgan toward the small rooms at the back.

Morgan hesitates, touching the worn sweatshirt of Kevin's. He knows it's not his actual skin, but he's come to love wearing it. It's soft and comfortable and it was Kevin's, and he gave it to him. His shorts he doesn't have any feelings toward—they're just to cover his body. Morgan still doesn't understand the human need for so many different layers, but he can respect the desire to appear different, to stand out.

"Hey, I'm not asking you to get rid of the sweater," Kevin says softly, stepping into the changing room with him.

It's a little cramped for two people, and Morgan stares at his reflection and Kevin's as Kevin slings his arms around him. "You always wear the same things, and I know we've washed them a few times, but I thought you might want to try something new and change things up."

Morgan smiles at him in relief. "Okay." He shrugs out of the sweater, folds it carefully and places it on the bench.

Kevin hands him shirt after shirt, laughs as Morgan changes, scrutinizes his reflection in the mirror. Morgan looks garish and washed out in bright colors, too somber in darks. They go through several piles of clothes.

"You look good," Kevin says, turning Morgan to the mirror. He's wearing a soft, sand-colored jacket, a muted green long-sleeved shirt and dark blue jeans, similar to the ones Kevin is wearing.

"I look human."

Kevin shrugs. "You look like you. Do you like the clothes?"

"I don't have any—" Morgan starts, realizing that Kevin always paid for their food when they went out. It hasn't felt strange until now, because Morgan always brought Kevin gifts as well—fish he had caught, or shiny rocks and baubles he found on the ocean floor. He realizes now, surrounded by all the things humans make for themselves, the intricate way they trade with one another for goods, that he doesn't quite fit in. He doesn't know how *he* would fit in. He's only here because he's with Kevin, fulfilling his Request for someone to spend time with. And Morgan loves Kevin, loves everything about him.

But Morgan doesn't have anything to offer other than his company. He's seen other human couples, walking hand in hand, making lives together. Kevin's parents have jobs they work at, teaching other people about the world, contributing to society, making money to pay for the home they share. And they have their children. They have Kevin.

How could Morgan even begin to do any of that? Sure, he's learned by leaps and bounds this summer how the human world works, but soon Kevin will be going back to school, and there are things he wants to do such as go to college and study geology. Where does Morgan fit into any of his plans?

"It's a present, dude," Kevin says, pulling Morgan out of his thoughts. He kisses him warmly on the cheek. "When's your birthday? We'll say it's for your birthday."

"On the next new moon I will be seventeen." Morgan starts to undress. There's something specific about this particular moon, something his mother told him was important, but he doesn't remember, not when Kevin's face is lighting up and grinning.

"When is that?"

"Ten days," Morgan says, thinking about the bright quarter moon that has followed him the last few nights as he swam back to the beach.

"Oh, so you *are* older than me. That's what I thought. You're turning seventeen! That's so exciting." Kevin's eyes sparkle as he hugs Morgan around the waist. "I don't know if your family does anything for birthdays? Do you have, like, a fish party on the beach?"

Morgan shakes his head and hands Kevin the jacket, shirt and jeans he's taken off. Right after he told him about being a selkie, Kevin was full of questions. *Where does your family live? Can you all turn into people? How come you're the only one allowed in town? What do your brothers and sisters do for fun? You said your dad is human; where is he?*

After Kevin realized his line of questions made Morgan uncomfortable, Kevin never brought up the subject of Morgan's family. Morgan hadn't known how to answer the questions about his father—he's never known him outside the stories, and he has no idea where he might be. He could tell Kevin was curious, though, and wanted to learn more.

"We don't have fish parties," Morgan says. "I don't actually know what you mean by that, but we do stay up all night and sing when a pup turns seventeen. It means you aren't a child anymore, but an adult, part of the herd proper, able to sit in on Council meetings and offer input on where to go and which Requests to fill. We keep track of age from year to year, but there aren't large gatherings like in the photos you've shown me of your celebrations when you were younger."

"Ooh, you're going to sing all night, that sounds amazing. I'd love to be there and hear all of you."

Morgan hesitates. No one has ever brought a human to any of their secret hiding places.

Kevin's face suddenly falls. "Ah, you said at night, huh. My parents are pretty open-minded, maybe a little too open-minded. If I ask if I can stay overnight at your place or something, it'll make them think we're doing something else."

"Like what?"

Kevin turns bright red, blinking, glancing quickly at Morgan's bare skin. He grabs the old sweatshirt and Morgan's shorts and pushes them at him, looking into the corner of the small dressing room. "Uh, I ah, it's not important. Anyway, I don't think they'd let me stay over, not unless they've met your parents or we've been dating a lot longer and uh yeah…" He stares under the door at a pair of feet walking by; the ripe scent of embarrassment lingers in the air. "Your birthday! That's awesome, I want to do something to celebrate! So like… this will be part of your present, but I have another idea and it will be a surprise, okay?"

Morgan gets dressed quickly, amused at how Kevin is rambling on about Morgan's birthday. He doesn't know why the amount of visible skin affects Kevin this way, but it's fun to watch his skin flush and his eyelids flutter.

Kevin leads them to the counter and pays for Morgan's new clothes, and they leave the store. Kevin's so excited that Morgan doesn't have the heart to say he can't take the clothes with him—where would he put them, if he swam with them to the hidden beach where his family stays? He could hide them in the same cove where he hides his pelt, but these are brand new clothes, gifts from Kevin. Morgan can't imagine leaving them in the cove, letting the briny salt water rush in at high tide and ruin them.

Kevin is saying something.

"What?" Morgan replies.

"Are you okay, Morgan? It's the mall; I thought you'd like it."

"No, it's fine, I just—can I keep the new clothes at your house? Could you keep them for me?"

Kevin blinks. "Of course—I can't believe I—I'm sorry, I didn't realize you wouldn't be able to take them with you. I just wanted to get you something—"

"No, it's fine. I like them a lot, thank you." Morgan takes Kevin's hand and squeezes it affectionately. "I can wear them when I'm here."

"Okay. Um—I was saying this shop sells fried cheese on a stick. Do you want to try?"

Morgan laughs. "Yeah, definitely, you know I love fried foods."

Hot dogs and cheeses are dipped in batter and deep fried in front of them. Morgan watches as the oil bubbles; the scent of hot batter wafts in the air. The cheese oozes, hot and melting inside its doughy container, when Morgan bites into it, and the fact that it's already on a stick is hilarious but amazing.

Kevin holds Morgan's hand as they leave the mall, and the whole trip and the lovely experience should be nothing but relaxing and satisfying, and it is, right up until they pass a clothing store decked with gaudy signs that read "END OF SUMMER SALE."

Morgan shudders, and he can't help the nervous feeling that runs through him, knowing that by summer's end the Request will be complete.

ELEVEN.

THE SUMMER DAYS are a flurry of activity: holding hands as they hike the trails, Morgan attempting to teach Kevin diving and swimming techniques, fooling around in the water, playing in the surf. But the best moments are small and intimate: the warm, open smiles that light up like the sunsets they watch, or the way their hands find each other, fingers curling together.

Afternoons are spent lounging in Kevin's bedroom until the light filtering through the west-facing window turns from gold to crimson and then fades into twilight. They cuddle, hands finding each other, fingers laced together, or with Morgan curling up in Kevin's lap, using his thigh as a pillow. They lose time kissing each other slowly. Kevin delights in how novel it seems to be for Morgan, teaching him to use his tongue, coaxing the prettiest sounds from him as they touch.

Morgan seems content with this and doesn't bring up sex at all, doesn't seem disappointed when Kevin pulls away before things get too heated. Kevin should probably check in with Morgan, but considering he turned as red as a tomato the first time Kevin suggested he *open* his mouth during a kiss, it's probably safe to assume they're all right on that front.

Kevin figures if Morgan wants to have sex, he'll bring it up. He seems perfectly fine with how things are progressing. And as long as Morgan's happy, Kevin's happy.

They hike all over San Simeon State Park during the next few weeks, holding hands, becoming such regulars that Jenny, the ranger by the front entrance, waves happily every time Ann's little car rumbles into the dusty lot with the two of them grinning at each other in the front seats. Kevin smiles fondly as Morgan gasps at the view from San Simeon Point, at the vastness of the ocean, at how the shore stretches on for miles. Morgan drags Kevin out into the ocean without his surfboard or his wetsuit, lets the waves barrel him over, teaches him to ride the waves as each incoming current splashes across them. It's exhilarating and cold, but Morgan loves it—and he never seems to want a wetsuit—so Kevin builds a tolerance to the temperature.

It never ceases to amaze him how fast Morgan is in the water, bobbing through the waves, swimming almost tirelessly, laughing and waiting for Kevin to catch up. At high tide one day, they swim back and forth, racing each other until they're out of breath.

Kevin teases Morgan when they're back on shore, accusing him of letting him win.

Morgan grins. "I'd never. You're a fine swimmer."

Sally looks up from her lifeguard post as they pass by. "You *are* really good. Not too many people can swim against the current like that. You on the swim team at school?"

"Nah," Kevin says.

"Well, you should be. Or consider trying out for junior lifeguards, you know. Could use someone like you."

Kevin shrugs, and Morgan throws him a supportive but curious smile. He'll probably have to explain what lifeguards and swim teams are once they're out of Sally's earshot, so he takes Morgan's hand, and they walk off.

"Say hi to your sister for me!" Sally calls after them; her tone is just a little too casual.

Kevin laughs and looks over his shoulder at Sally, who is pretending to busy herself with her chemistry textbook.

"What is it?" Morgan looks from the now blushing Sally and back to Kevin.

"People are funny, that's all," Kevin says. Sally and his sister, that's interesting. He wonders if Ann knows, or if this was a thing when they were in high school that she's never talked about.

"Oh yes, I love your jokes."

Kevin is pleased; he always gets reluctant groans from his family. "Knock knock," he starts.

Morgan laughs immediately, and Kevin feels like the luckiest boy in the world.

ONE AFTERNOON MORGAN asks Kevin to meet him at the beach; his excited grin hints at a surprise. Kevin spots him as he steps across the sand, which is warm in the late sun. He passes a group of hikers with a lot of strange equipment. From a distance Kevin thought they were weird—dressed for a backpacking trip, with large packs and trekking poles, instead of the more casual wear the beach joggers usually favored.

But, closer up, the things he thought were trekking poles look like modified metal detectors. One instrument buzzes strangely, and a man with salt-and-pepper hair waves a map excitedly at his group. The only instrument Kevin recognizes is the Brunton, and he's annoyed when he realizes the man holding it is using it wrong.

They're definitely not geologists. Kevin's pretty sure they're the same group he spotted at the cafe, hikers who wanted to show off their outdoorsy prowess with equipment they didn't understand. He remembers one of them adamantly denying they were geocachers and that they were doing "science," but what kind of scientist purchases a Brunton without learning how to use it? Kevin doesn't understand what they're doing with the metal detector, either. *Whatever.* He's got a boyfriend who's got a surprise for him.

Morgan waves at him from the edge of the beach, grinning.

Jogging past the hikers. Kevin calls out, "Sorry!" when he accidentally kicks sand at one of them.

He overhears the hikers conversation as he passes them:

"Him?"

"No, he's a local. His parents are both professors at the state college."

"Still… he could…"

What a weird thing to say. Maybe they're students taking a class, not hikers. There are many field courses going on this time of year. That seems more likely.

Kevin puts the encounter out of his mind when he hugs Morgan. Morgan laughs, presses his face into Kevin's neck and kisses Kevin wetly on the cheek.

"All right, what do you want to do?"

"You said you would like to meet my family. I thought we could go on a journey." Morgan holds up the sealskin. It almost glitters in the sunshine. The darker spots shift as Morgan shakes it, blacks and grays blending together in fluid motion.

"Can I?" Kevin asks, reaching for it. He hasn't seen the sealskin since that night Morgan told him his secret.

Morgan offers it to him, and Kevin takes it reverently, awed at how much trust Morgan is giving him. "Beautiful," Kevin says, holding it up. "Would I make a good seal?" He throws it over his shoulders and smiles at Morgan.

Morgan laughs at him, bumping him with his hip. "You're too skinny to be a seal." He pokes cheerfully at Kevin's arm. "Not enough fat. You'd get cold easily. That's why you need extra skins when you are in the water. Come, let us go."

Kevin twirls exaggeratedly, the pelt flapping about him like a cape as he follows Morgan to the water. "Obviously it looks better on you." He admires the pattern of the spots on the pelt and has a sudden thought, looking up at Morgan's bare back. He's got freckles, a myriad of small dark spots, dancing down his shoulder blades and his spine, disappearing under the shorts Morgan is wearing. Kevin holds out the sealskin, grinning as he compares the spots to those on Morgan's back. They're a match, of course.

He follows Morgan into the waves, holds the pelt aloft, walks until the ocean floor drops out beneath his feet. Morgan is already treading water, waiting for him out in the depths, bobbing in the waves. Kevin wraps the sealskin carefully around him like a scarf and swims out to Morgan, breathless with excitement. He unwraps the pelt and hands it to Morgan, taking a careful glance back toward shore. The people on the beach and the lifeguard tower look like toys; Kevin can barely tell what they're doing, so it's probably safe for Morgan to transform here.

When the next wave comes in, Morgan drapes his pelt over his shoulders and closes his eyes, concentrating. In the time it takes to inhale, a gray dappled seal looking right back at Kevin. Morgan jerks his head as if to say, *Let's go.*

At first Kevin just treads water, confused, and then Morgan swims circles around him until Kevin laughs and pets his head. Morgan makes a pleased noise and nudges him closer, and Kevin throws his arms around Morgan's sleek neck, and then Morgan dives ahead in a rush of blue-green water.

Kevin hangs on as Morgan swims up the coast at breakneck speed. Kevin laughs delightedly as the wind rushes past his face, whipping his hair back. They speed toward the horizon; the sun sparkles on the water and the ocean stretches out to forever. They pass the rookery, where tourists are snapping photos of the seals basking in the sun, then head north.

Kevin isn't sure how long they've been swimming, but the sun is hanging low in the sky, and he can't see any buildings on the coast. They come upon another beach, which is flanked on both sides by impregnable cliffs. Kevin can't see a trail leading down to this beach; if there is one, it's well hidden. He supposes one could hike down to the beach if one knew it was here, but the way the cliff is eroded away at the base would make the shoreline impossible to see from above.

Morgan swims ashore, and Kevin can see a few seals sunning themselves near the water. Something about them strikes him as different from the seals at the rookery: a shimmer in the air around them, an intelligence in their eyes.

Morgan barks out a greeting. A small, chubby pup waddles over, making happy noises in return.

Kevin climbs off of Morgan's back and Morgan slips out of his sealskin, then steps onto the beach with him. The young seal transforms into a naked toddler, and excitement colors his brown cheeks to a deep ruddy red. He runs forward; his pelt falls into the sand as he rushes to greet them. The boy hugs Morgan around the knees and laughs.

"This is my younger brother, Marin," Morgan says, ruffling his hair.

"Hello, I am Kevin."

The boy smiles, hiding behind Morgan's legs, blinking big green eyes at him.

"He's not normally this shy." Morgan shrugs. "I've been telling him about you all summer. He's a big fan of rocks, too."

Another seal, larger, with a solemn expression, slowly moves in front of them. She transforms into a woman with a regal expression, and drapes her pelt around herself like a cape.

"Kevin, this is my mother."

Kevin manages a bow similar to the one Morgan gave him when they first met, trying not to show how embarrassed he is that she's naked. Her sealskin is covering a lot, but she's still—*oh gosh, this is mortifying.* Kevin has no idea what to do, but reminds himself that casual nudity is probably normal for selkies. Morgan trusts him enough to bring him to meet his family, to show him where they live. Kevin needs to make a good impression.

"I am Linneth," she says in a voice as melodious as Morgan's. She is tall, with a thin nose and curling, reddish-brown hair tumbling past her shoulders. She has the same brown eyes as Morgan, but where his are wide-set, innocent and curious looking, her eyes are narrowed, scrutinizing Kevin. Linneth is both beautiful and terrifying, and Kevin tries to seem less nervous and focus on her face.

A quick glance around the beach shows at least twenty more seals and a few pups, some on the rocks, and some in the water. Kevin is quite certain the rest of the seals on this particular beach are also selkies; their intelligent eyes look on with interest, but no one else shifts.

"My son has told me many things about you," Linneth says.

"Good things." Morgan smiles and pats Kevin's shoulder in assurance.

Kevin nods nervously.

"Are you having a good summer?"

"The best," Kevin says. "Morgan is… he's the most incredible person."

Linneth smiles at him, and Kevin breathes a sigh of relief.

Morgan tugs on his arm. "Come on, I want to show you some rocks I think you'll like. And then we can sing for you."

The cliff does look interesting, and any other time Kevin would have loved to study the striations exposed in the rock, but today he's in the company of selkies. *Magic.* "Thanks for thinking of me, but this formation will probably be similar to the one close to home. I'd love to hear you all sing, of course. Morgan said you plan to sing all night for his birthday?"

Linneth fixes him with a strange look. "In a few days my son will turn seventeen. On the night with no moon, under the stars, he will come into his heritage. We will sing until the stars give way to a new morning, for the inevitable change."

It's an ominous way to talk about one's coming of age party, but Kevin isn't going to judge anyone's customs. "Sounds great."

Kevin looks at Morgan, and he gets a small nod in return, as though Morgan is nervous about it. It's probably a big deal for selkies, and Kevin gives him a supportive smile, which Morgan returns, relaxing slightly.

Morgan says something to his mother in another language, which Kevin recognizes from the song he sang for him, in which words slip over themselves like bright water in a bubbling brook.

She raises her eyebrow, nods, and responds with a short few words and then her voice carries out, strong and clear across the beach, catching the attention of the other seals.

They come forward; some of them shift into human form, bodies human but eyes glinting with a wild curiosity. Pelts are flung across shoulders or wrapped around laps or laid out on a rock. Kevin tries to focus on their faces or stare off into the distance or even look only at Morgan, and once again reminds himself that his discomfort is just a by-product of being raised in a society where clothes are normal. *I'm the weird one here.*

Kevin relaxes as the selkies talk to one another, gathering nearby, clearly excited about whatever Morgan and his mother are planning.

Kevin notices that they're all either much older or much younger than Morgan. He's the only teenager—of those who've shifted into human form, three look as if they're in their late twenties. An attractive young woman with dark blonde hair tumbling softly in wet curls down her front sits next to Kevin and gives him an appraising look.

"Naida," she says, flicking her hair over her shoulder.

"What?" Kevin blinks at her, and then blushes and looks away from her bare torso.

"It's my name." Naida shoots him an unimpressed look. She pats the empty patch of sand next to her until Kevin sits down.

"Oh! You're Morgan's sister."

Naida grins mischievously, and Morgan nudges her warily. "Do not—"

"Please, it's my little brother's boyfriend," Naida says, voice tinkling like bells. "I've been hearing about you all summer. Is it true you have a special shrine for your rocks and each of them has a name?"

"It's a display case, and the specimens do have labels, but it's not like they're my pets or anything…"

Morgan huffs and shuffles off to talk to another selkie, someone who has shifted into a male close to Naida's age who pulls him away with a barrage of questions.

Naida focuses her startling green eyes intently on him. "Kevin, I'm just letting you know—"

"I'm not going to hurt him," Kevin blurts out. "He's the best thing that's ever happened to me. You don't have to do the older sibling talk with me, okay? It's not a quick summer fling or something like that. I really want to—I really see myself with him in the future. Like, this year I'll be doing college applications and stuff, right? I figured he might want to go with me—he's not bad, the way his SAT practice scores have been. I mean, he'd need to work on his math, but his verbal score is pretty good. Which is pretty cool, you know. He told me about all the knowledge he gets from the Sea, and he's already really smart, so I don't think it would be a huge push for him to try for college. And I can ask my dad for help with his paperwork or something, build a paper trail of grades and stuff to show?

"Or, um, even if he didn't want to apply to college, he could go to community college, too. Like, you don't need to have prerequisites or high school transcripts? And it'd be neat, since Morgan wants to do marine biology. I figure he can transform anytime and swim with the fishes... or eat them, I dunno. I think he might like it, whatever it is..."

Naida looks sad all of a sudden. "He would. He's always been a curious guy, and he's had many strange theories about why fish do what they do, and go where they go..." She sighs, then bites her lip. She opens her mouth to say something else, but Morgan returns before she can.

"I think we're going to sing the story of Berend." Morgan's eyes glitter in excitement. "It's a little bit like your Mr. Darin's song. It's about losing love and finding it again."

"Okay," Kevin says. He's comfortable sitting on the sand, crossing his legs, feeling the sun warm his skin. His swimsuit is already starting to dry, and the selkies come closer to him.

Of those who are in human shape, some have similar features, but if Morgan hadn't told him they were his family, Kevin never would have guessed. Maybe they're not all related? Naida's features resemble Linneth's, but are different from Morgan's. The selkies' skin tones range from pale, like Linneth and Morgan, to tan, like Naida and a few others, but Kevin can see a number of darker-skinned selkies as well. Does this herd have selkies from all over the world?

A few toddlers like Marin curl up in laps in their human form, and others waddle around as chubby pups, nosing at an adult until someone strokes them affectionately. One of the pups crawls into Morgan's lap, and he laughs. The pup curls up contentedly, blinking at Kevin.

Kevin waves and smiles, and the seal hiccups. His pelt tumbles off his chubby little body and he turns into a toddler with flyaway black curls. The toddler waves back and tugs the pelt around himself like a blanket.

Linneth clears her throat and smiles. She sings; her voice is a high, resonating alto, the first note light and playful. The other selkies join her—those in human form and those as seals—and it's a bright, happy tune.

Kevin listens, watching the mingled joy and happiness. He can feel it: the emotion of finding love, finding companionship. The sentiment seeps into his skin, as it did when he listened to Morgan sing, now multiplied by a force of twenty. Each voice finds another in perfect harmony, and even if Kevin doesn't understand the language, he can follow the story.

Linneth sings the main part about her character finding joy and happiness, and another selkie sings the lover's part, voice weaving with hers. There are meetings with friends, pieces of the story told by the others, more characters are introduced and then there is a misunderstanding, and the lover has to leave. Linneth closes her eyes. Her voice is clear and strong, and everyone looks up to her, especially Morgan.

Then the song turns sad and longing, and Kevin feels tears well up in his eyes.

Morgan nudges his shoulder, takes his hand and squeezes, and Kevin shakes himself. The song ends and there's a murmur of approval. Kevin isn't sure what to say when many questioning eyes turn toward him. "That was beautiful. I could feel—feel the music in my bones, the happiness, the sorrow." He bobs his head in deference. "Thank you for letting me be here."

"Of course," Linneth says softly, her words tumbling over one another prettily. "My son is happy. What more could I ask?"

Something about the way she says it seems strange to Kevin, but he forgets when Morgan, beaming at him, leans over to kiss his cheek. And then he drags him over to the cliffside to see the unique rock face, and Kevin forgets about everything other than Morgan's hand in his and his smile as they explore the area.

Twelve.

IT'S QUITE LATE by the time Morgan swims back after taking Kevin home. The moon is high, a thin sliver gleaming against the dark. Morgan lets the tide wash him onto the beach. He hums happily, transforms on the shore and skips across the sand. Feet are so much fun to walk on, and Morgan's making up for the lifetime of keeping to his seal form by enjoying the feel of sand on his skin, the cool air brushing past his hair.

"It doesn't take that long to swim to the Moon's Eye," says a voice to his right.

"Good evening, Micah."

Micah steps out of the shadows, his pelt draped across his shoulders, his arms crossed in front of his chest. "Did you have fun?" he asks, grinning lewdly at Morgan.

Morgan blushes. "We kissed," he mumbles. "It was nice."

Micah saunters forward. "I spent last summer on a Request." He leans into Morgan's space, his finger arched above Morgan's neck where just moments before Kevin kissed him eagerly. It felt nice, and Morgan sighed into the touch, wondering if he should do the same, if Kevin wanted him to touch him elsewhere.

"You know the old stories of why we go ashore for Requests."

"Yearning hearts. We all know the stories." Morgan swats Micah's hands away.

"The landwalkers, the lonely ones, would cry their hearts into the Sea, or their longing would carry across the distance, and we would hear it. And someone would go there and ease that loneliness."

"Yes? What are you getting at?"

"Oh, you silly pup. Have you not mated with this Kevin of yours yet?"

Morgan almost trips over nothing. "What—that would be—"

He thinks about the mating he knows, of seals undulating against one another on the beach, sand flying everywhere, cries of passion. He knows humans do something else—he's seen a lot of movies with Kevin where hc assumes the characters mate with each other, but with everything they've watched so far Morgan can only think of it as kissing. Horizontally? Does Kevin want to do this?

Morgan's cheeks heat up. "I don't think that's part of his Request. He wanted someone to spend time with. That's what I'm doing."

Micah bumps him on the shoulder. His eyes are fonder than Morgan remembers, and he realizes Micah hasn't said anything rude or teased him about his human heritage. "I mean for you, aren't you curious how they do it? It's fun, you know."

Morgan thinks about one of the movies they watched, where the lovers embraced passionately. He and Kevin kissed for a long time after that, moving around on Kevin's small bed, bodies close together, skin warm and hot, and Morgan is curious why sometimes Kevin springs away, flushed with embarrassment. It's obvious to Morgan that it's about mating, and he's a curious, especially remembering the diagrams and pamphlets and supplies they'd looked at, but Kevin never seems to want to talk about it, just gets completely flustered and changes the subject to hiking or going out to eat.

"Okay, maybe I'll ask him about it," Morgan says. It's clear that Kevin is shy about the idea, but it might be good to ask if it is something he wants to do.

"Good." Micah smiles again, relaxes his posture.

Morgan narrows his eyes. "Why are you so interested in my mating habits?"

Micah shrugs. "Just looking out for you."

"When I was a pup I got caught in a riptide and you were laughing the whole time."

Micah shuffles his feet, eyes downcast. "Well, Naida pulled you out; you were never in any danger. And it was funny—but okay, you're right. That was wrong of me. I just—I want you to experience everything you can, you know."

"Okay…"

Why is Micah looking at me like I'm breakable?

Linneth appears behind them, the looming bulk of her seal form silhouetted against the scant moonlight. "You don't have to tiptoe around it anymore, Micah," she says softly. "I'm going to tell him tonight."

"Tell me what?" Morgan asks, not able to help the note of fear that crawls into his throat.

Micah sniffs, lurches forward, and hugs Morgan suddenly, clasps him tightly to his chest. Morgan pats his back awkwardly.

"Your mother is looking for you," Linneth says to Micah, who nods and walks off.

Linneth jerks her head forward, and Morgan follows her back to the shoreline. She wades into the water; Morgan transforms into a seal and follows her around the cove.

"Now the rest of the herd can't hear us. How was the rest of your night with Kevin?"

"It was fine," Morgan says. "What's going on? You haven't done midnight swims with me since I was a pup."

Linneth rubs a flipper fondly over his head. "Do you remember why we stopped?"

Morgan flops onto his back, floating, watching the stars. "The others accused you of playing favorites."

Linneth makes a humming noise. "It's true. You have a special place in my heart, always." Her voice is soothing, like the cool water brushing over him, familiar and safe. The night sky stretches out dark and infinite; stars gleam in the distance, singing their songs far away. She splashes him playfully. They swim together, circling one another, and it's easy to pretend Morgan is a child again, with no worries at all, just the waves brushing past him, his mother swimming alongside him, the stars blinking above. It's a warm, comfortable silence, but he can't fully enjoy it, knowing there's something she needs to tell him.

Finally Morgan blurts out, "So what do you need to tell me? Does it have something to do with why Micah's trying to be nice to me now?"

Linneth sighs. "Oh, my darling. I never wanted this life for you."

Morgan turns to look at her. "You mean the Request? But you told me it was an honor to be chosen by the Sea…"

His mother shakes her head. "No, that is an honor, and you're doing wonderfully—I just—it's my mistake, and I'm sorry that you'll have to—you'll have to…"

Morgan is surprised to see his mother break from her normal composed self, tears welling up in her eyes. "Mother, what—?"

"Morgan, you must know that the Sea has long discouraged any mingling between those of the Land and the Sea, especially for us selkies, considering our ability to interact with the humans, even to walk amongst the landwalkers in secret. The Sea is a possessive, jealous mother, and never wants us to forget our own heritage. There was a treaty made long ago: We keep to our own realms outside of Requests and our blood should never mingle. If a child was born of such a union, that child would live, but only until their seventeenth year."

Morgan flounders, his body dipping below the water's surface. He splutters and comes back up for air. "I'm going to die?"

"No. You will have to choose. Live as a seal, or live as a human. You cannot be both."

"That isn't fair."

He's always found the Sea's thrum of magic comforting, the way the knowledge sinks into him whenever he asks, but he feels betrayed as he listens to a whole history of halflings who grew to seventeen years of age and were given a choice—stay as a human, lose all memory of the herd they grew up with, or remain a seal, never able to shift again.

The Sea has little information on those who took the human path, only that they forgot about having been a selkie. It also becomes clear why he's never met another halfling—no, wait, Morgan *has*. There was that one herd with a seal that they treated like family. Morgan had been confused at the time, but she must have been a halfling who had made her choice.

The enormity of what his mother isn't saying sinks in—why Micah was being nice to him, why everyone in the herd listened carefully to his stories.

"I know it isn't fair," Linneth says. "I am sorry. I would not have—I was selfish, and kept you for myself. It was a time when I wasn't sure I was ever going to be able to return to the Sea, and I thought, if I must be trapped forever on land, having a child would be so—" She sighs as if lost in her memories. "He was excited about the baby, as was I, and we were happy for a little while, but I couldn't forget that it wasn't my choice; he made that choice for me. I don't think I ever forgave your father for wanting to keep me beyond the terms of his Request."

Morgan waits, listening. He's never heard her speak so openly about his father before.

"He was a fisherman. Quite handsome, with a sharp sense of humor. I loved him, and he wanted me to stay. I think if he had asked—" Linneth sighs again, her body undulating as she swims along. "It doesn't matter, because he didn't."

Suddenly, Morgan is angry at his father. Even though he's heard the story so many times, his mother has never said so much about this man's effect on her life. And *his* life.

"You were born here, on this beach." Linneth looks towards the hidden cove where the other selkies are settling in to sleep for the night, just shadows on the sand. "I was too pregnant to swim very far when I left, and ended up here. I brought us back here because I thought, if you chose to be human, you should have resources. I don't know of many halflings, but most have chosen to remain seals, stay with the herd. But you've always been strange, hunting on your own, swimming far. And though you never shifted until this summer, I knew there was a chance you might want—"

"I don't want to leave my family."

"If you stay a seal, you won't ever be able to shift again. You won't be able to see Kevin, or talk to him at all."

Morgan falters, and he swims ahead, angrily making his way through the waves and the otherwise peaceful night. Why can't he have everything? Be able to see Kevin whenever he wants, shift whenever he wants?

"Morgan." Linneth swims up to him quietly and extends a comforting flipper to his back.

"The Sea says if I'm human I won't remember," Morgan says, choking up. "I won't know you or any of the herd and I won't remember Kevin, either, so what's the point?"

"A chance, if you want it. There are dangers, those who would harm us and other supernatural beings. You would be safer if you didn't remember. And you wouldn't be alone."

"What are you talking about?"

"Do you think it coincidence that I brought our herd to summer here? A place I haven't visited in, say… seventeen years?"

It takes a moment for Morgan to realize what she's talking about. "My father. You're saying he lives here. In Piedras Blancas."

"If you choose to live as a human, he could—I could ask him to help. I know he would. You wouldn't have to be helpless, with no memory of who you were or who you could be. They have things, writings, ways to record—"

"Yes, I know. You think there's a way he could help me remember who I was?"

"You won't be able to remember you were a selkie. But you could make a note of Kevin, your feelings…"

Morgan sighs. "When do I have to choose?"

"The new moon."

"That's in four days." Morgan looks at the barest sliver of light hanging in the sky. "Kevin asked me to—he wanted to do something special on Saturday, he said for my birthday, the way humans celebrate it."

"That's fine. Go spend time with your lover. It is the end of the summer anyway, and the end of the terms of your Request. Say goodbye. Or tell him to find you when you see him again. Whatever you want to do, it will be fine." She looks resigned, as if she knows it won't be, and Morgan can see the same bittersweet glimmer in her eyes that she used to have when talking about his father. He wonders if she's already decided to think of Morgan as lost. "I only want you to be happy."

Morgan wants to cry, to ask how he could be happy if he's being forced to make this impossible choice—if he could have Kevin, but not his family, or vice versa. He keeps silent, though, knowing that look on his mother's face, knowing she's close to tears and doesn't want to cry in front of her son.

His mother places a gentle kiss on his forehead and swims back to shore, letting Morgan stew in his own thoughts.

He looks up at the dark sky, swims on his back, listens to the Sea whisper around him, as if the Sea is waiting for a question, ready to give him more information, more stories of what other halflings have done.

Morgan has so many questions. Why had no one told him sooner? Would his decision to take the Request have been the same had he been told at the beginning of the summer? But for the first time in his life, Morgan doesn't ask—he doesn't care what the Sea knows.

Morgan's certain that before meeting Kevin he would have accepted just being a seal. He wouldn't be able to shift, but since he'd never shifted before, he wouldn't have minded. And he would still be able to be with his family. He would not be able to talk to his family as he could now, but he would still be around.

But now? He knows the Request is only for the summer, and then the herd will leave, following the current to wherever his mother decides to take them for the next few months. It has always seemed possible that Morgan could return to Piedras Blancas, the next summer maybe, and see Kevin again. At the very least, he could tell Kevin goodbye and promise to return.

But this? Morgan will be a shell of himself, whatever he chooses. As a seal he would get to stay with the family, swim and hunt, live out the rest of his days with them, but he would be like—he would be mundane, as he understands it.

And as a human? With no memory? Even if his father agreed to help, would he be the same person?

"What do I do?" Morgan asks the night sky.

The stars wink back at him, and there is no answer.

THIRTEEN.

KEVIN IS EXCITED about Morgan's birthday. He doesn't want to make the same mistake he did when he bought him clothes at the mall. Spending time giving Morgan the best possible experiences of the human world will be far more valuable to him. The county fair will be great—lots of people to watch. Morgan will like that. Plus, all the fried foods he can eat, the games, the rides.

Kevin can't believe he'd forgotten about the fair. The flyer came in the mail a few weeks ago and it completely slipped his mind until Morgan told him about his birthday.

Morgan hasn't shown up this morning. That's okay. Sometimes he spends time with his family doing seal things. Kevin grins as he jogs to the beach. *My boyfriend is magical.* He says it to himself again, pleased that he's entrusted with such a huge supernatural secret. Kevin's been doing a pretty good job of keeping that secret so far. His parents are both incredibly nosy—well-intentioned, but nosy. They've dropped hints about wanting to meet Morgan's parents, asked what they do for a living, where they're staying.

Kevin doesn't enjoy lying to his parents, but he understands the need for secrecy, so he has done his best to give evasive answers as close to the truth as possible, letting them draw their own conclusions. He said that Morgan's family was "at sea," which his dad took to mean they owned a boat. Kevin tried to come up with an explanation for why they weren't at the docks, but didn't get further than saying that they were avid fishers, and his dad just nodded, guessing that they were currently anchored somewhere north of town. Kevin might have to ask Morgan if it's okay to tell them the truth, but right now Kevin's more interested in daydreaming about taking Morgan on the Ferris wheel.

Kevin jogs down the beach, watching the waves roll in. He catches his breath at the lifeguard tower, intending to say hello to Sally, but she isn't alone.

Three other people sit in the sand in front of the tower, listening intently as Sally reads from her clipboard.

"Kevin! Hey! Trying out for junior lifeguards?"

"Uh, just going for a jog." Kevin nods at the others, recognizing the tall black girl and the shaggy-haired blond guy next to her, but not the third person. Michelle and Connor were in his English class last year. He might have seen the other guy with the soccer team. Kevin's seen all of them around town before, but he's never tried to socialize with any of them.

"You totally should. There's enough money in the year's funding to train and hire four people. Plus I've seen you swimming and bodysurfing all summer; you could totally do it." Sally bumps Kevin with her hip, causing him to stumble a little.

The guy on the end laughs. "Hey, I'm Patrick. Totally bump her back, dude. She did it to all of us."

Kevin hesitantly bumps his hip back against Sally, and she snorts a little at his daintiness, but the three sitting on the ground cheer politely. "I guess having a job would be nice," Kevin says.

"Fantastic," Sally says. "Have a seat."

TWO HOURS LATER, Kevin is completing his first group interview session, scheduling a CPR class and has a bunch of new employment forms to take home to puzzle over.

"Hey, you live on my street, right?" Michelle asks, with her flyaway corkscrew curls bouncing as they start walking toward town.

"Yeah." Kevin has seen Michelle on his bus, but he's never talked to her before.

"We can totally walk back together. Connor rode his bike and won't let anyone sit on the handlebars because he's a safety nerd—"

"Hey!" Connor snaps on his helmet. He makes a rude gesture toward Michelle, who turns around and mirrors it, laughing.

"You're taking AP history this year, right? We should totally be study buddies. I hear Miss Tran does pop quizzes every week. We can totally go over stuff on the bus ride to school," Michelle says.

"Yeah, sure," Kevin says.

Connor whizzes by on his bike, waving and hollering, and Kevin feels out of the loop when Michelle and Patrick shout back at him. The feeling is fleeting, though, because they're soon talking about studying for the SAT and the Marvel movie that's coming out next year. Michelle is a DC fan, so this sparks what seems to be an old argument between her and Patrick as Kevin watches, amused, not wanting to get between them.

"You're pretty cool, Kevin," Patrick says. "Just goes to show certain people at school don't know what awesomeness they're missing out on."

Kevin makes a face. "Let me guess. You've heard what Skylar's been saying?"

Patrick nods. "Yeah, I mean I left the soccer team because he was being such an idiot about me being in the changing room. Not that I would ever look at his pasty ass."

Kevin knits his eyebrows together in confusion. "Wait, you're—"

"Gay, yeah," Patrick says. "I didn't come out until after you did, though. Didn't see what the big deal was about telling people, but I used to be friends with the dude, and I wondered if he'd do me the same as he did to you. So, yeah. I think he would have, if my mom wasn't the principal, but I think I got the least of it. Just some snide remarks from him. And since he was team captain, the other guys just kind of followed suit."

"Sorry to hear that."

"I'm not. Michelle convinced me to join the swim team, and I'm having way more fun there. Plus we actually win our competitions, unlike the soccer team."

"Whoa," Michelle says, halting them in the middle of the street. "Who is that? I thought I knew all the cute guys who live in this town."

Patrick turns and follows her gaze, then lets out a low whistle.

Kevin spots Morgan casually walking on the other side of the street, apparently on his way to Kevin's house. He's wearing only his board shorts as usual; the line of his bare back is visible as he walks. Then he turns, noticing them. Morgan's face breaks out into a smile when he sees Kevin, and he waves at them.

"You know him?" Patrick asks.

Kevin grins. "Yeah, that's Morgan, my boyfriend."

"YOUR FRIENDS SEEMED very nice," Morgan says when Kevin finally manages to pull him away. Morgan walked up to them, and then Kevin introduced them, and then Michelle and Patrick had more questions than Kevin was sure Morgan was comfortable with: where he went to school and where he lived. They also seemed fascinated when Morgan talked about swimming, though, so luckily the conversation went in that direction. "Michelle remarked that she wished she had the courage to walk around in her swimsuit like I am. I get the feeling it was meant to be flattering, but somehow also not."

Morgan pokes his stomach, staring at himself, and Kevin sighs. "Hey, some people are just self-conscious about their bodies. Don't take it the wrong way. I think Michelle was impressed you're so confident, and you're not like… Mr. Six Pack or anything."

Morgan's eyebrows knit together. "I don't know who that is."

Kevin considers explaining, but Morgan is probably better off without being saddled with the insecurities that might come from the explanation. "Don't worry about it; you're the hottest selkie I know," he says, leaning in for a kiss. "And they both thought you were great, so it's all fine." He takes Morgan's hand, squeezes it tightly and walks with him toward his home. In the distance, Michelle and Patrick wave goodbye.

"I'm glad to see you making friends," Morgan says. "I feel a lot better, knowing you won't be lonely."

"Yeah, I guess. I mean, I always kept to myself at school. I figured having one friend was enough, but I guess he wasn't really a friend. Or anything else, really."

They walk past Miles' house, and Kevin can see him in the upstairs window, glancing out to the street. Kevin thought seeing him would be weird, or that he'd feel vindicated somehow, or he'd want to rub it into Miles' face that he's moved on. Kevin hasn't felt any such thing, and now doesn't have the urge to do anything other than keep walking to his door with Morgan.

They go to Kevin's bedroom. Morgan usually sprawls out comfortably on the bed, but today he's standing by the wall.

"Hey, are you okay?"

"Yeah, I just—I wanted to tell you something."

"Is everything all right?" Kevin has a sudden, terrible thought. "Your family's okay? Those hunters didn't figure out where your beach was, did they?"

"No, nothing like that, I…"

Kevin pats the bed next to him, and Morgan sits down. He takes a deep breath; worry is written all over his face. Kevin slings his arm around his shoulder, pats him and strokes his thumb over Morgan's shoulder in a repeated, comforting motion.

Morgan looks up and gives him a small smile. "I—um, I found out my father lives in Piedras Blancas."

"What? Really?" Kevin is surprised, but calms himself down, looking to Morgan for an appropriate guideline on how to react. Morgan doesn't seem excited about it, or angry, and Kevin's not quite sure what to do. Should he be comforting? Encouraging? Go for a hug?

Morgan's jaw is set. "My mother wanted to give me the option of meeting him. If I wanted to. That's why we came here this summer."

"And do you want to?"

Morgan looks ahead. "I should. I really want to ask him a few things."

"Do you know who he is? Need help finding him?"

"His name is Richard, and he was a fisherman. That's all I know. I suppose I could ask my mother to track him down, but I don't want her to know I went to see him before…"

"Before what?"

Morgan shakes his head. "It's not important."

"Okay, well, if you want to talk to him, he should be pretty easy to find. I'm sure someone will know who he is; it's a small town. And you say he's probably lived here the entire time? Since before you were born?" Morgan nods, so Kevin stands up. "All right, I'm gonna ask my parents later, if that's cool. They can definitely help you out."

Kevin's parents are still at work, so Kevin opts for putting on a movie instead of studying. Morgan picks *The Little Mermaid*, which makes Kevin laugh, but they watch the Disney movie anyway. It's a cute movie. Kevin hasn't seen it in a long time, but he remembers all the songs.

As usual, watching Morgan enjoy the movie is the best part. He laughs at the portrayal of mermaids, shakes his head disparagingly when the movie shows the glorious city of Atlantis and his eyes widen when Ariel makes her deal. During Ariel's foray into the human world, though, instead of bombarding Kevin with questions, Morgan falls quiet.

When the credits roll, Kevin looks at Morgan's pensive face and brushes up against his shoulder hesitantly. "Did you like the movie?"

"I don't know." Morgan grips the sheets on Kevin's bed, with his hands tight in small, frustrated fists. "I don't think that situation would have happened in the first place. If Ariel had wanted to explore the human world, she wouldn't have been shamed for it. At least not if she were a selkie. It might be different for merrows. I only know of them from stories, and they don't care for humans much at all."

Kevin thinks about the story Morgan told him earlier in the summer, about the wounded merrow singing desolately for her lover, dying in vain as he drowned. "I can imagine why," Kevin says dryly. "This particular story is made up, though, for fun. You know, mostly for kids to see a happy ending and true love conquer all, and all that."

"It doesn't always."

Kevin stares. He's never seen Morgan get upset, not since his pelt went missing, and it's a weird thing to be upset about, a lighthearted kid's movie.

"Hey, hey," Kevin says, pulling him in for a hug.

Morgan trembles slightly, but he holds on tight. Kevin feels hot, wet tears drop onto his back. "Do you want to talk about it? Is it the merrows? It's sad because what happened to them in real life is a tragedy, and the story makes you feel…"

Morgan shakes his head, and Kevin holds him, feeling the beat of his heart against his chest, waiting for Morgan to open up.

"I just think it's not fair," Morgan says finally. "I—people should get happy endings."

"Come on. You're thinking about that sad story you told me, aren't you? Look, there's nothing we can personally do to change any of that. But what we can do is focus on ourselves. Hey, I can tell you about my surprise."

"Surprise?" Morgan pulls back to look at Kevin.

"Yeah, for your birthday. You're turning seventeen the day after tomorrow! I have something totally awesome that you're gonna love. I'm gonna take the whole day and we're gonna drive down to SLO and I'm gonna take you to the county fair. It's a gathering of people, just to have fun! There will be rides and games and so many fried foods. You're gonna love it!"

Morgan nods at him; the corner of his lip quirks up a little, even though sadness remains in his eyes. He hugs Kevin again, presses his face into Kevin's neck, breathes deeply. "Thank you, Kevin. It's really thoughtful of you to think of something I'd like. It sounds like a lovely way to end the summer. I'm…I'm looking forward to it."

Kevin strokes Morgan's back, glad that Morgan is excited about the fair, and starts talking about cotton candy and how amazing it is, in hope of drawing him out of the mood even further. Morgan nods and listens, holding on tight to Kevin. Cuddling isn't new for them, but this time Morgan doesn't want to let go. Kevin doesn't understand, but he's happy to stay in the embrace until Morgan lets go.

FOURTEEN

MORGAN HAS THREE days left to decide his future, and he is no closer to knowing what to do. Kevin has been adorably concerned, though he assumes what's weighing on Morgan's mind is only the idea of meeting his father for the first time.

The next morning, Kevin has something to show him.

"It took me forever, but I got it. My parents didn't know anyone in town named Richard, so I had to resort to the Internet, and no number of keywords with Piedras Blancas or California and Richard or fishing turned up anything useful. But then Ann was going to the Cambria Public Library to return her books, so I hitched a ride, and I talked to this nice lady about microfilm and newspapers, and I found this!"

Kevin brandishes a piece of paper at him so excitedly that Morgan can't tell what's on it until Kevin calms down and lets him look properly. It's a copy of an issue of the *Piedras Blancas Gazette,* from about twenty years ago. There's a photograph of a young man with broad shoulders and a happy smile, proudly holding a huge flounder aloft. "The Pride of Piedras Blancas," Morgan reads slowly. "Cal Poly biology graduate student Richard S. Floyd set a state record yesterday, catching a twelve pound starry flounder during the Annual Western Outdoor Fishing Tournament."

"I can't believe it's him," Kevin says, shaking his head at the photo. "I always thought he was weird. I'm sorry if that's mean. I feel bad for thinking your dad was weird, now."

"It's okay."

Morgan studies the photo. Floyd's handsome, full of life and beaming at the camera. Morgan thinks about the time he and Kevin ran into him at the park. Time has not been kind to him.

"I asked my dad about Old Man Floyd, and he says he lives past the lighthouse. Do you want me to go with you?"

Morgan shakes his head. This is something he has to do on his own.

KEVIN ALSO THOUGHTFULLY prepared him a map of where Floyd lives, on the outskirts of town. It isn't difficult to walk there. The warm sun beats down on Morgan's skin, and he hears the laughter of tourists making their way through town, snapping photos of the seals on the beach. Morgan passes them by, watching the families smile and walk, wondering if this is a small respite from their own busy lives and if any of them have ever had to make a choice like his.

"Hey, you live here, right?" a girl asks him. Her friends watch from a few steps away.

Morgan is caught up in the question, thinking about where he *lives*. It's a human concept, one he's always thought strange: home as a concrete place. He's sure if he'd ever been asked this before, his answer would have been, *No, I live in the Sea,* but that's not completely right. Home is the waves, his family swimming beside him as he hunts for fish, the sparkling water and the hidden depths, forests of kelp swaying gently in the current. But home is also Kevin's smile, the way he cuddles up next to him in Kevin's bed, watching movies; it's the colorful rocks on the trail in the state park, the dazzling cliffs and the beaches.

"Do you know a good place to eat?" she presses on, jolting Morgan out of his thoughts.

"Yes." Morgan gives her directions to the cafe he and Kevin once visited, so long ago. "They have fish and chips, and sandwiches too. The French fries are good."

"Thank you!"

Morgan can hear her talk to her friends as he continues to walk and wistfully imagines their lives for today: spending time together; enjoying the sights; going out to eat. Here he is, about to talk with a father he's never met in hopes of getting insight into a decision that will change the rest of his life. The sunny day and jovial tourists do little to change Morgan's dark mood.

When he reaches the outskirts of town, he follows an unkempt trail to a dilapidated house. He supposes it could have been a beautiful little cottage overlooking the sea, with a lovely view of the Moon's Eye, or the lighthouse, as Kevin calls it. The house looks terribly lonely, with faded blue paint peeling off the shutters and long-dead roses still standing by the path. If Morgan didn't know someone lived here, he would guess it was abandoned.

Morgan sighs, pockets the map and raises his hand to knock.

The door swings open before his fist meets the surface, and a grizzled man with a dark beard coarse with gray hairs peers out at Morgan.

"I don't want to buy anything," he says, scowling.

"That's not why I'm here. You are Richard S. Floyd?"

"Yes." Floyd narrows his eyes. "What's this about?"

"I am your son," Morgan says, with more calm than he knew he had. "May I come in?"

"YOU LOOK LIKE her, you know." Floyd gives Morgan a scrutinizing once over. "Can you—are you like her? Can you do the thing?" He waves his hand in a vague gesture.

"I am a shape-shifter, yes, if that's what you're asking," Morgan says flatly. He's beginning to wonder if this was a mistake, coming here. Floyd takes the news readily, needing no more than Morgan's brief explanation. The description of Linneth and their lives is enough. It seems Floyd is hungry for someone, anyone, from that world to confirm what he has believed all along.

Floyd's house is small and cramped, filled with knickknacks, and smells strongly of fish. Yellowing photographs cut from newspapers hang on the wall, picturing Floyd in his youth, handsome and striking, standing proudly and holding aloft various large fish.

"Why are you here? Did Linneth send you?"

"I just found out. And, no. She doesn't know I'm here."

"She's… here, then? Close by?" The question lingers in his eyes, which sparkle with desperate hope.

"I don't know if she wants to see you or not. We've never summered in this area."

It's a half-truth, but Floyd doesn't need to know that. He seems too keen to know his mother's whereabouts, and if there's anything Morgan has learned from all the movies he's watched with Kevin, it's that having a bargaining chip can be helpful. His mother said she would want to talk to him, if Morgan chose to be human, but giving Floyd this information now might change his mood and make him utterly unhelpful. From what Morgan remembers of their one encounter on the beach, he is impulsive, quick to anger, and Morgan doesn't want to leave here without answers.

"Look, kid—"

"My name is Morgan."

Floyd jerks forward; his hand reaches out as if he wants to touch Morgan's face, to see if he's real.

"That was my father's name. I didn't know if she—" He laughs to himself, but it's a dry, mirthless, hollow thing. "For years after, I wondered if that time with her was a dream. We were happy. And then one day she was gone, just like that. I always wondered what had happened, if she had the baby, if the two of you were out there somewhere. Or if something worse…"

Floyd hangs his head in shame. He pulls out a photo from a drawer in the rickety desk in the corner: a cracked thing, well-handled over the years, stained, probably by tears. In the photo a younger Floyd stands with his arm around Linneth, grinning at the camera. Linneth is blurry, caught in the middle of a moment, head tilted back in laughter, looking not at the camera but at Floyd. Morgan looks at the photo and shakes his head when Floyd offers it to him, and Floyd returns it to its spot in the drawer.

This bitter old man, hands dirty with grease, living in this cluttered hovel, is not the father Morgan imagined. He thought he was a handsome, dashing man who stole his mother's heart, convinced her to stay with him and then selfishly tried to keep her for himself. Morgan thought he would be scary, maybe, like a villain out of an old story. That man *was* in a few of their family's stories—none of the popular ones, since he always made his mother sad, but Morgan remembers his aunt singing one in particular, painting with her words a picture of a terrifying, selfish man, cruel and larger than life.

This man just seems sad. Morgan almost feels sorry for him.

"You tried to keep her," Morgan accuses, and Floyd nods.

"I loved her. I knew she was pregnant when she left, I just—I didn't know if you would turn out like me, or like her, or some combination of both. I knew all the stories, and I just wanted us to be happy. Like a family. I would have tried my best, you know. To be a good father to you."

Floyd reaches for Morgan again, and Morgan lets him hesitantly pat him on the shoulder.

"It was selfish, what you did. You hid her sealskin so she couldn't return to her true form. After that, how could she trust you?"

Floyd's eyes brim with tears. "I only wanted her to stay."

"You should have asked," Morgan replies coldly. "But we don't have time to reminisce about the things you should or shouldn't have done. I need your help."

"I don't have much money. You're welcome to whatever I have. I don't know what use any of it would be to you, under the Sea."

It's a small gesture, and Morgan wants to be grateful, but the desperate situation he's in, not knowing what to do, fills him with so much frustration and anger that he stands up, fists clenching. He wants to lash out, to take every single knickknack in the house, throw them on the ground and break every last one of them into little pieces, then seize the trophies and photographs and throw them out the window.

But that won't solve anything.

Floyd watches him, and if he notices the tears falling from Morgan's eyes, he doesn't say anything.

"It's not fair," Morgan says finally. "You—and my mother—you did this. And I can't, I can't be the way I am anymore, it's this stupid magic—I just—"

The words tumble out of him, ugly, hot tears falling heavily down his front.

He tells Floyd everything.

At the end of the story, Floyd pulls from of his pocket a single white handkerchief, possibly the only clean thing in the house, and hands it to Morgan.

Morgan sniffles into it, wiping his tears.

"For what it's worth, I'm sorry," Floyd says gently. "I didn't know about this rule. I don't think I would have pushed Lin for a baby if I'd known. Guess it makes sense now, why she didn't want to at first."

Morgan stares at him, thinking of his mother's wistful staring out into the night sky, wanting a child for company, hoping for happiness in a difficult situation.

They sit in uncomfortable silence. Floyd doesn't offer any more comments, or advice, or even an opinion on which choice is better. Morgan waits, but Floyd just looks at him with a mixture of disbelief and regret.

Finally, Floyd speaks up, voice cracked from disuse. "Glad to see you're okay, been okay this summer, knowing what you are. Ain't exactly safe for your kind right now hereabouts."

"What, the hunters? We've known about them for ages. I'm the only one allowed on land for my Request; everyone else is to stay in the Sea."

Floyd nods. "They're not all a bad bunch, but there is one guy, Nathaniel, who's always been set on catching one of you. He even tried to get me to come with, for old times' sake."

"You—you knew, wait—you were one of *them?* You hunt us and still—"

Floyd blinks at him. "It wasn't like that. There are some who are overzealous, yes, but I was a scientist. We all were. Most of us were simply fascinated by the stories and the magic in the deep, or knew someone who knew someone who had a relative who had an encounter, and we would have been thrilled just to learn more. In more recent years, the pursuit has become less about knowledge and more of a *hunt*, if you will. I stopped associating with those fools after I met Lin. I realized they wanted more: to capture them, document proof and share it with the world. I dropped out of my graduate program, stopped traveling with them, settled down here and took up fishing."

Floyd shuffles to a bookshelf in the corner and pulls out an old, leather-bound journal. He flips it open, showing Morgan detailed drawings, some familiar—selkies, merrows, a kraken—and some completely new to him, drawings of people who sprout fangs and fur. Morgan wonders if these are some of the beings Kevin talked about when he first told him he was a selkie.

"It doesn't matter. The herd is leaving soon anyway," Morgan says. "The summer is pretty much over, and after I choose…"

Floyd pats him awkwardly on the shoulder. "If you decide to be human. It sounds rough, not remembering anything. I don't know how, but if I can help—in any way—I'll try."

"I'd like that. Thank you."

"The least I could do. Missed out on being a father to you all these years. I could at least start now. I messed up with your mother, I know. I was afraid she wouldn't want to stay. Who would give up the wonders of the Sea for me and my little house? But you're right. I should have asked."

He sighs, looking at his feet, and then squares his shoulders, as if he wants to start being fatherly right now. "Been seeing a lot of you on land, though, this summer. You still with—"

"Kevin," Morgan says, a knot of worry forming in his gut.

"You care about him."

"I love him."

"Would you stay on land? For him?"

Morgan knows it's not part of the Request, the question of him staying forever. It doesn't mean he hasn't thought about it, about what it would mean, getting to be with Kevin all the time instead of traveling south with the herd when the summer is over.

"I would," Morgan says. "If he asked."

FIFTEEN.

KEVIN IS IN the kitchen gulping down a glass of orange juice. He grins when he sees the flyer for the county fair in San Luis Obispo pinned to the refrigerator. It's the last day of the fair. He's planned this just in time.

"Ann!" he yells. "I'm borrowing your car today, remember?"

His sister looks up from her seat in the living room, puts down her book and raises an eyebrow. "What, you're not gonna go surfing with your boyfriend?"

"Come on, Ann, please, I really wanna take him to the county fair and today's the last day. It's his birthday."

Her eyes crinkle in amusement, and he knows he's won.

Ann tosses the keys at him. "Remember to fill it up with gas when you're done. Don't have sex in the backseat; I'll know if you do."

Kevin blushes. "Ann! We're not doing that."

Ann laughs at him. "Uh huh, and you guys spend all that time in your bedroom with the door closed just for fun."

"We hang out! Movies and things!"

A few times kisses have gotten heated, and Morgan's dislike of clothes means in private he's usually very close to naked. Kevin's a teenage boy; Morgan is very attractive; it would be difficult *not* to be aroused even if he were clothed all the time. It's not that Kevin hasn't thought about it, but it is a difficult thing to ask. Plus, Morgan is so *innocent* about so many things. He figures if Morgan ever wants to, he'll let Kevin know. Until then, he's more than happy with what they have.

"Right," Ann says. "Have fun. Win me the biggest stuffed animal you can."

The doorbell rings, and Kevin finishes his juice quickly. He rushes to the door, smiling widely at Morgan, who is wearing Kevin's sweatshirt and the orange shorts again. "Hey!" Kevin says. "You're probably not wearing anything under that." Poking the collar down reveals skin, as he expected.

"You realize I'm still sitting right here," Ann says.

Kevin rolls his eyes. "Here, I'm gonna get you the clothes you left in my room."

Ann's eyes widen. "I'm *still* here!"

Kevin's cheeks heat up, but he knows whatever he says Ann will find a way to turn into a joke, so he just runs up to his room. He realizes the shirt they bought is long-sleeved and made out of a thick blend. Morgan will probably be more comfortable in something else, since it's going to get warmer later. He digs in his dresser, laughing when he finds a T-shirt with a smug-looking cartoon seal with the words "SEAL OF APPROVAL" printed on it. Dashing back downstairs, he finds Morgan chuckling at something Ann is saying.

"What are you two talking about?" Kevin asks, narrowing his eyes.

"Nothing," Ann says. "Giving Morgan some advice, that's all. Have fun, kids!"

Kevin glares at his sister, and she gives him a jaunty salute. "C'mon," Kevin says, taking Morgan by the hand and pulling him into the downstairs bathroom, ignoring Ann's scandalized snort from the living room.

Morgan looks as cute as ever, waiting with a slightly confused expression. Kevin hands him the jeans and then holds out the shirt. "Here, what do you think?"

"It is a comical representation of a seal." Morgan unzips the sweatshirt and takes the shirt. He gets stuck pulling it on.

Kevin pulls the shirt over his head, careful to not tug on Morgan's hair. "What was my sister saying to you?"

"She was asking about our mating habits."

Kevin cheeks heat up. "Um, right, our, ah, mating habits."

"I told her not to worry. You have a full day planned at this fair, and I reassured her that we would not be mating in her vehicle."

"I hope you're not mating in the bathroom, either!" Ann's voice resonates through the wall, sending both Kevin and Morgan into fits of laughter.

THE DRIVE IS fun. Pop songs blare on the radio, and Kevin sings along, making Morgan laugh hysterically at him. They pull into the fairground and park alongside the throngs of people, all eager to enjoy their day. "This is going to be great," Kevin declares, buying a generous number of tickets.

Morgan is awestruck at everything: the popcorn, the cotton candy, the bright colors, the chiming music playing constantly and the people everywhere. He gets cotton candy all over himself; pink floss sticks to his lips and cheeks, and Kevin has to kiss it away. Once again he feels warm contentment at being able to kiss in public, hold hands with Morgan, who is without insecurities or qualms about being seen with him. They're happy and in a relationship, and Kevin could scream it to the world and Morgan would just smile that sweet, happy smile.

They go on the Tilt-A-Whirl first—Morgan shrieks delightedly as the ride spins them in dizzy circles—then head straight to the Flying Chairs. Morgan's eyes widen when the machine lifts their swings up, higher and higher, and he grabs Kevin's hand.

"It's totally fine, look!" Kevin says, pointing out the view of the city. Then the swings spin, and their feet dangle in the sky.

Morgan is breathless when they get back to the ground and he shakes his head. "That was incredible!"

"There's more rides, but do you want to try any of the food? There is, like, deep-fried everything you can think of."

Morgan's eyes light up and they make for the food booths, where they purchase deep-fried Twinkies. Morgan sighs around the sweet mouthfuls and his eyes glaze over. It's so adorable that Kevin gives him his share as well. *This is never going to get old.*

"Don't you want some?"

"Nah." Kevin kisses him. Morgan tastes like buttery cake and cream. "I've got the best dessert right here."

Morgan's eyes crinkle up, and he tries to kiss Kevin but starts laughing. Kevin can't help but laugh as well; he loves his puns and cheesy one-liners. He never thought he'd be comfortable saying them out loud, he's so used to having to self-edit because no one appreciated his weird humor. Morgan does, though, and Kevin adores that about him.

They spend a few hours playing the games. Kevin knows they're rigged, but they're fun to try, and he's got plenty of tickets to spare. Morgan tries and tries to toss a plastic ring onto a bottleneck, and they spend so many tickets at the booth that the operator takes pity on them and gives them one of the smaller toys, a stuffed octopus that makes Morgan laugh.

"They are so much larger than this," Morgan says, holding the toy in the palm of his hand.

A funnel cake later, they're tired and full. Kevin counts their tickets; they've got enough for one more ride for the both of them, so he pulls them onto the Ferris wheel.

Inside their car, Morgan rests his head on Kevin's shoulder. Contentment is written all over Morgan's face as he settles in. The wheel brings them higher, and Kevin wraps an arm around Morgan's shoulders, resting his head on his.

"This was so much fun," Kevin says. It might be the best day he's had all summer.

"Thank you for bringing me here. I've never done any of these things before, would never have gotten the chance if I hadn't met you."

"You're welcome." Kevin presses a kiss to Morgan's forehead.

Morgan curls himself into the embrace, and the car rotates again. Now they're at the top of the Ferris wheel, with the entire fair spread out below them and the ocean sparkling far in the distance. Morgan burrows his face into Kevin's neck. "I love you."

It feels right, in this moment, for Kevin to take Morgan's chin and softly tilt his head up, and then to capture Morgan's lips in a gentle kiss, smile, and say, "I love you too."

Morgan makes a little noise of happy surprise, and then he wraps his arms around Kevin and doesn't let go until the ride is over.

They hold hands the entire car ride back. Morgan falls asleep; his head falls forward, bobbing with every turn of the road; his chest rises and falls peacefully. Kevin keeps his eye on the road, a hand on the steering wheel and one hand clasped around Morgan's. The smile on Morgan's face seems a little sad, but Kevin can't think why. Is it because it took him all summer to feel comfortable enough to say how he feels, to acknowledge that he does love Morgan? It's a happy thing, right?

Kevin parks the car at the beach and gently pokes Morgan awake. "Hey, we're back."

"Oh."

Kevin was right; Morgan does sound sad. Maybe it's just that the date is almost over.

They exit the car, and Kevin grabs his backpack, feeling around to make sure the container inside is still intact. He takes the blanket out of the trunk as well, and holds his hand out to Morgan. "One last birthday surprise."

Morgan takes his hand and they walk onto the sand. Kevin rolls out the blanket and pulls the plastic container from his backpack. The icing melted a bit while they were at the fair, but otherwise it looks fine: a clumsily made lemon and poppy seed cake covered in white frosting.

"I made this for you," Kevin announces.

Morgan takes the container; his eyes widen as Kevin pulls a single blue candle from his backpack. There are matches, too, and he grabs a different package by mistake looking for them, and blushes. Kevin makes sure he has the matchbook, checking for the rough texture of the striking surface before he takes it out.

He strikes a match and lights the candle, then holds the little cake aloft in front of Morgan. "Make a wish."

"A wish."

"Like a Request. It's a human birthday thing. Make a wish, blow out the candle, eat cake."

Morgan closes his eyes shut. "I wish—"

Kevin places a finger to his lips quickly. "No, don't tell me. Otherwise it won't come true."

"Okay." Morgan shuts his eyes again.

Kevin waits, and it takes some time for Morgan to think. The little birthday candle is burning quickly to a stump, and Kevin's about to pull out another candle to give him more time, when Morgan suddenly opens his eyes and blows out the flame.

Morgan's chest is heaving, his eyes sparkle and he looks at Kevin, with a face full of hope.

"Happy early birthday, Morgan," Kevin says softly.

Morgan moves closer, and Kevin is about to reach for the plastic cutlery in his backpack so they can eat the cake, but Morgan kisses him, surprising him with the rushed intensity of it. The kiss is desperate, hungry, and Kevin gasps when Morgan seizes him by the waist, pulling him closer.

He returns the heated kiss with enthusiasm; his heart pounds as Morgan presses him to the blanket, Morgan's body is heavy against his own. Kevin's out of breath by the time Morgan pulls away and looks up at his flushed face and shining eyes.

"Is this okay?"

"Yeah, absolutely," Kevin replies, reaching out to stroke Morgan's jaw.

"I don't know how to, I've never, um, but I want to—I want to mate with you," Morgan says, his face red. "Do you want to? Do you know how?" Morgan's voice wavers, betraying the confident way he's almost sitting on Kevin's lap.

Kevin thinks about the condoms and the lube he stuffed in one of the backpack this morning, just in case. "Yeah," he says gently. "I can show you."

The night sky is gleaming with stars, with the barest hint of moonlight from the last sliver of the waning moon, and Morgan almost seems to glow; his skin is luminous in the dancing light of the waves. Kevin is aware of the twinkling constellations and the gentle blue calm of the ocean undulating behind them, but out of all of them, Morgan is the most beautiful.

SIXTEEN.

MORGAN MEANT TO make it a proper goodbye, meant to tell Kevin everything, that after today they would never see each other again, that it would never be the same. But the day was so perfect, and Kevin told him he loved him, and made that beautiful sweet cake and sat with him by the beach in the moonlight, and Morgan *wanted*.

And it was wonderful, like falling apart and being put back together, with nothing but the music of the ocean, the soft sounds of Kevin's breath and the warmth of his body under him.

Kevin fell asleep, after, and Morgan lay there in his arms, listening to his heartbeat and thinking. There was no point in *both* of them having a broken heart. Surely Kevin would think of Morgan's disappearance as coinciding with the end of the summer, and he would be sad and miss Morgan, but he'd known what he was getting into when he'd made the Request, the terms he had made with the Sea. He doesn't need to know about Morgan's specific circumstances, and Morgan can spare him whatever frustration or anger he would have had over Morgan's choice.

Morgan closed his eyes to rest, to curl up contentedly on Kevin's chest, to tangle his legs between Kevin's own, to feel warm and happy and safe.

He didn't mean to fall asleep, but there's soft light behind his eyelids now, and he opens his eyes to see the dawn's light over the horizon.

A new day. Morgan's last day.

Morgan nudges Kevin and whispers, "Kevin."

"Mmph," Kevin mumbles and tugs Morgan closer. His hand finds Morgan's and squeezes it fondly.

"You should get home before your parents and sister wake," Morgan whispers, repeating Kevin's own worries about staying out late.

"Huh? Oh, yeah." Kevin sits up and blinks wearily. His hair sticks up in all directions, and it's unbearably cute. He smiles when he sees Morgan sitting next to him, and they dress hastily, fumbling and blushing, throwing looks at each other. Oh, what Morgan would give to explore this further, to have more of Kevin laughing at him, kissing him, holding him close!

He tries to keep it together as they pack everything up, but Kevin seems to notice something's wrong.

"Hey, are you okay?"

"I'm fine," Morgan says a little too quickly, because he sees Kevin's face fall.

"Last night—"

"Was amazing," Morgan finishes. A smile blooms on Kevin's face, and Morgan doesn't want to bring up any of his own issues. Not now, not after a perfect day. "I'm afraid my family's party won't be nearly as fun." *Yeah, not fun at all, just an elaborate ritual at midnight where I'll be irrevocably changed.*

"Aw, are you singing the main part or something? It's your birthday, of course. Well, I'm sure your solo will be amazing."

"I don't even know what I'm going to do," Morgan mumbles.

Kevin shrugs, and even though he has no idea what they're talking about, his words ring true anyway. "Just follow your heart."

"Thank you." Morgan leans forward for a hug, and nearly falls apart in Kevin's arms. More than Kevin will ever know, Morgan will be forever grateful for this experience. Kevin hugs him tight and finally lets him go. He helps Morgan back into the sweatshirt, and Morgan fondly recalls Kevin giving it to him on this very beach. It feels forever ago, and Morgan can't help the tears, so he pulls the hood up and yanks on the drawstrings, tightening it until it frames his face and covers his eyes.

Kevin laughs, and kisses Morgan on the nose. "You are the cutest."

"Goodbye," Morgan says. It would be selfish to say more, he thinks. Better to let this be a last good memory for Kevin.

Kevin kisses Morgan again, this time on the lips, and Morgan wants to make it last forever, but he can't.

"See you later!" Kevin says, walking back toward the car, as casually as if this was just another day, and he would see Morgan tomorrow.

Morgan watches him drive away, and Kevin turns around once. Morgan, alone on the beach, waves, and Kevin waves merrily back.

Morgan lets the tears fall, now that Kevin is too far away to see.

THE WINDS HAVE changed, and it is officially autumn now. While the California coast remains warm, Morgan can taste the colder air soon to come as he swims back toward the beach. He sleeps for a while, but his body is restless, and there are still many hours before the decision needs to be made. Morgan still isn't sure what to do, and knows he can't meet with Kevin again since the terms of the Request are over. But it doesn't mean Morgan can't see Kevin, as long as Kevin doesn't know he's there.

"You made a decision?" Micah asks as he watches Morgan get ready to swim. "You're gonna stay with us, is that why you're getting in as much landwalking time as you can?"

"I don't know, Micah," Morgan snaps as he dives into the water. Micah follows, swimming next to him like a shadow. "Why are you following me?"

"You can't see loverboy again. Is that where you're going? Didn't get enough mating in yesterday?"

"How would you even know what we—ugh, I'm not answering that—what is your weird obsession with mating, anyway?" Morgan splashes water in Micah's face.

Micah makes a pleased sound. "Aw, little Morgan's all grown up. Proud of you, cousin. Although I can't say the same for where you're going now. You know it's over, right? What are you gonna do, go *look* at him?"

"YES!" Morgan snaps, stopping suddenly and glaring at Micah. "After tomorrow, I won't be able to—at least not in the same way! And he won't understand, and I can't bear to tell him. What if he thinks it's his fault, or he does something stupid to try to change it. It's all set in stone and terrible, no matter what I choose!"

"I'm sorry. I mean, not just for now, although I was kind of a kelp-head. I didn't get it, you know, you being a halfling. I just thought it was funny. I shouldn't have made fun of you when we were growing up. I didn't know until this summer, what it meant, you know." His voice turns solemn. "It sucks, what you have to do. The choice, I mean."

"Thank you." It doesn't make up for years of teasing, but it's nice to know Micah is trying, at least.

Another shape swims toward them, and Morgan is surprised to see his mother, who rarely ventures out on her own. "Hello, boys. Best we all return to our beach; hunters were spotted out on the beaches near town today."

"But—"

"I know you want to see Kevin, but you can't. It would violate the nature of the Request, and we can't have an angry Sea. Come along," she says, guiding them both forward.

Micah follows, making an apologetic gesture at Morgan, who shakes his head and swims after them.

A small hunting party is getting ready to leave on the beach, and Morgan thinks it would be a good distraction, but Naida stops him. She shares a look with their mother, eyeing Morgan as if he's something fragile. "Go on ahead," she tells the others, who slip into the waves. Naida takes Morgan aside, nuzzling at him. A flipper pats fondly at his side, and she sighs a little.

Morgan opens his mouth to speak, but she holds up the flipper. "Don't tell me what you decided," she says.

Morgan falls silent. He doesn't know how to handle this moment—they should be reminiscing, laughing, sharing a story or something, but after his outburst with Micah he is emotionally exhausted.

Naida nudges him, and just sits silently with him like when Morgan was a pup, waddling after her in the sand, stopping to listen to the wind.

"You'll be fine," Naida says finally. "You're smart, and resourceful, and whatever happens, you'll still be you."

"I'll miss you," Morgan says. It feels childlike to admit it, but it's true.

Naida huffs, but he knows she's smiling.

There's nothing to do on the beach after Naida leaves, and Morgan is listless after an entire summer filled with activity with Kevin. The hunting party is gone, and no one is in the mood for singing, so there's nothing to do except laze about in the sun.

"Why don't you transform for a while, spend some time in your human form," Linneth suggests.

Morgan doesn't ask why she thinks he's already chosen to stay a seal, but he follows her suggestion, slips out of his pelt and lets it dry on the rocks near some of the pups' pelts. They laugh and play in the sand, no life-changing decisions hanging over any of their heads. Morgan doesn't join them; instead he walks out to the rocks and sits there silently on his own.

Morgan closes his eyes, listens to the wind rushing past him and the waves crashing down on the shore, tastes the salt in the air. It'll be difficult, giving up this form, now that he knows what it can do, what the sensations of the human body are, how everything is so bright and colorful to his eyes. But to stay human? He would miss the way sound plays on his skin, sending him the voices of his loved ones like a comforting embrace. He would miss the endless stories of the Sea, available at a moment's notice, and the joy of rushing ahead toward the horizon, swimming aimlessly, or even snapping up fish in his jaws.

Morgan sighs. Maybe he'll just decide tomorrow on a whim. Kevin did that once, taught him about chance by flipping a coin. He doesn't have any coins, but he's sure he can figure something out.

He sits up on the rock, stares at the horizon and wonders what Kevin is doing this very moment.

Seventeen.

KEVIN IS LAZING about, eating his bowl of cereal slowly, when he realizes it's past the time Morgan usually stopped by. Maybe he should meet him at the beach.

Kevin puts on his wetsuit and grabs his surfboard; he whistles to himself as he takes the short walk to the shore.

A few joggers run past him, but other than that the beach is empty.

Kevin frowns, walking from the pier to the lifeguard tower to the cave, but Morgan is nowhere to be found.

"Morgan?" Kevin calls out, his voice carrying across the beach. "Morgan!"

He doubles back to the lifeguard tower and sees Sally putting on a layer of sunblock. "Hey, have you seen Morgan?"

"Haven't seen your boyfriend around, kiddo."

Kevin frowns. "I'll come back tomorrow. Let me know if you see him today."

"Would do, but I won't be here. Alex will be on duty, though. I'm starting classes tomorrow at Cuesta; fall quarter starts early, ugh. You guys at the high school aren't starting 'till after Labor Day, right?"

"Wait a minute," Kevin says, blinking. The summer is basically over… and he…

He didn't even realize.

"I have to go," he mutters, running off.

What did Morgan say yesterday?

It's been a fantastic summer. Thank you for bringing me here. I've never done any of these things before, would have never gotten the chance if I hadn't met you.

Kevin stares at the pier ahead of him. How could he have forgotten? It was what he asked for when he shed those seven tears. He walks slowly, trying to remember the exact words and failing. Kevin was so happily distracted by Morgan, by falling slowly in love with him, that he forgot about the supernatural circumstances in which they met.

Kevin sets the surfboard down on the pier and breaks into a run; the memory comes back now as he races to the end. How could he have been so stupid as to ask only for one summer to be in love?

The tears come easily, fast and hot, tumbling down his face. Kevin hadn't believed it was possible; he made the wish on a whim, a memory of something his mother had once said—

Mom.

Maybe she knows something.

Kevin races back home, heart nearly pounding out of his chest. He flings open the door, bursts into the living room and sends papers flying.

"Kevin," Rachel scolds, dropping the red pen in her mouth, grabbing for the papers.

"Mom, I need your help."

She looks up, taking in his sweaty, disheveled appearance and panicked expression. The papers get pushed aside. "Are you okay? Come here, sit down. What's wrong?"

Kevin takes a deep breath, and somehow she knows without him saying anything.

"Ah, I see. You're usually out collecting rocks or surfing with Morgan this time of day. And now… you're not. Everything okay?"

Kevin shakes his head. "He's gone, Mom. I don't know—I think he was only here for the summer—"

"That's terrible. Want me to get us some ice cream? You look like you could use some."

"No—no ice cream. I want to—um, can you, like, distract me? With a story?"

"A story?" She laughs. "Okay, what kind of story?"

"You told me one once about, um, seven tears at high tide? And granting wishes?"

"Thinking about wishing yourself a new boyfriend? Thought you were pretty dead set on this one."

"No, no, um, just felt like hearing the story." Kevin sits down at the counter and props his chin on his hands.

"Well," Rachel says, taking off her glasses to regard him. She tucks a strand of brown hair behind her ear. "I remember my grandmother telling me this one, when I visited her one summer. She grew up on the Orkney Islands, and I think as a kid I always thought the place was bleak, but as a teenager I appreciated how beautiful and lovely the landscape was, the way the sea—"

"Mom. The story."

"Are you sure you're all right? I'm not sure this is the best distraction for you; these tales usually end quite sadly."

"Please."

"All right. How does it go… There was a lonely young woman whose friends had all married, and she was the only one of her age in the village who had not yet found a husband. There was no one she fancied at all, and she walked out to the shore at high tide, speaking of her sorrows, weeping into the sea. The seven tears that dropped into the water carried her yearning request to the heart of the sea, and then a seal came ashore and approached the woman, shed his skin and became a man."

His mom's eyes have a faraway look, and Kevin knows she can be long-winded. "Yeah, and they get together and they're happy for a while, and then he goes back. What happens after?"

His mom blinks. "I think that's how the story ends. After her husband finds the sealskin she was keeping hidden, he returns to the sea, and she mourns his loss. Why would you ask me to tell you this if you keep interrupting me?"

"Sorry, I just—I forgot this part. She hides the pelt to keep him human, but are there any stories where, like, the human doesn't do that?"

"Not that I know of. Like I said, most of these end sadly. I can tell you another story, where my grandma was sure she had met a brownie—"

"No, that's not what I—" Kevin sighs. He's not sure what he's looking for in these stories.

"I think there might be one story where a man had a selkie wife and every seven years she would come back to shore?"

Seven *years*.

Kevin steps away from the kitchen, shaking his head in dismay.

"Okay, maybe not that. Hmm, there's another one that also starts with seven tears at high tide—wait, that ends with them separated as well—wait, is that what you're looking for, a story where the two don't end up together, but it's comforting instead of sad?"

"What's going on?" His dad enters the room, glancing between them.

"Oh, Morgan moved away and Kevin wanted some stories to make him feel better—"

"Oh, you always loved the stories of the Monkey King when you were a kid," Mike offers. "I think we still have the VHS tapes. I can go set that up and we can watch those together if you like!"

Kevin sighs. "Thanks, Dad, not really in the mood for adventure stories right now, though. I'm—I need to be alone now."

Is there a rule about making more than one Request? None of the stories had mentioned that—and if they never said he couldn't. Maybe if he asked, Morgan could come back.

Kevin dashes out of the house, running for the ocean.

KEVIN HOPES FERVENTLY it will work once more. The tears drop into the ocean below, and he counts carefully to seven, then steps back.

"I want Morgan back," Kevin declares to the sea. "Please, if he wants to—if he wants to come back, I love him."

Another wave passes by, crashing past the wooden support beams. Kevin stares miserably at the water, watching the next wave roll on by, and then he decides to sit down, his body slumping to the wooden planks in defeat. Kevin gives up and lies back, looking dejectedly at the sky. It's not even cloudy, but a bright cheery blue, another beautiful day that Kevin doesn't get to share with the one person he wants to be with most.

A minute goes by, and then another. Kevin doesn't even know how long he's been crying here, lying down at the end of the pier like an idiot.

"That much is true," a voice says.

Kevin springs up and wipes his face, then turns to face the water. It's her—Morgan's mother. She's treading water, her pelt draped regally across her shoulders.

"Hello," Kevin says, bowing his head. He tries to keep his lip from wobbling. "Um… you heard my, er…"

"Darling, you poured so much emotion into that cry it's still resonating across the Sea," Linneth says.

"I love Morgan." Kevin holds onto the pier's railing for support. He feels like an idiot; all those times Morgan told him how he felt, and he never said it back. Well, once, but Morgan deserved more, to hear it every day—

"I know you do." The melodic lilt of her voice rises and falls in the same cadences as Morgan's, and Kevin is struck by a sudden pang of longing. "You asked the Sea for one summer, and you've had your summer to be in love."

"I didn't know any of this was real then! Magic, shape-shifting seals, none of it!"

Linneth hums, narrowing her eyes at Kevin. "You love my son. If he were human, you would love him still?"

"Of course."

"He was happier with you than I've ever seen him. Every night he would tell all his brothers and sisters stories of Above and his adventures with you."

Kevin's grip on the wooden railing tightens. *Where is she going with this?*

"Do you remember the beach where you met our family?"

Kevin nods.

"We don't plan to leave for the long swim south until tomorrow. You should come by. Approach quietly on foot. Around noontime today, some of us may shed our skins to walk in the sun on two legs. I have the feeling Morgan will want to spend time in his human form while he can."

"What are you saying?"

"Take his pelt with you, and Morgan will be bound to you as a human as long as you keep it safe and hidden from him."

"I can't just—steal him!"

"Others have been stolen before," Linneth says softly. "By humans less honorable than you. The two of you would be happy, I think."

And with that she slips away into the waves, and in the blink of an eye is a sleek seal, swimming away.

* * *

KEVIN CAN'T BELIEVE he's here, that he borrowed the car to find a hidden beach he's seen only once before. He can't look it up on a map, but relies on memory and some quick calculation of how fast Morgan swam that day and how much time passed on the journey from the rookery to the beach.

Parking the car off the highway, Kevin slips through chaparral, hikes slowly down to the beach, hides in the shrubbery as he gets closer to the sand. He can see the selkies beached in the sun and lazing about in the shallow water. A few are in human form, most of them children: chubby toddlers running around on their little legs, giggling and laughing and falling over in the sand.

Kevin takes in a deep breath when he sees Morgan sitting on a rock, staring off into the distance.

The pelts are all lying on the rocks. Even if the rest weren't too small, Kevin would still be able to pick out Morgan's pelt by the distinct gray-spotted pattern.

He creeps up to the pelts unnoticed and brushes his fingers along the edge of Morgan's pelt. Kevin looks up at Morgan's figure. Even though Morgan has a sad expression, Kevin's heart swells with affection. In an instant, he knows: *I can't do this.*

Kevin is ashamed of himself for even considering stealing Morgan's pelt. He made a promise that he would never try to keep Morgan for himself; he is going to keep it. He steps away from the pelts, slinks back into the shrubs and pauses to watch Morgan. If this is the last time he sees him, he wants to savor it, to memorize the angles of his profile, the curve of his jaw, the freckles on his back.

Kevin remembers what Morgan once said about love, about wanting that person to be happy. He knows forcing him to come back wouldn't be right. Whatever happens now, even if the rules of the Sea say they can never meet again and it was only for this one summer, Kevin knows he's still grateful to have known Morgan.

"Goodbye," Kevin says quietly from his hiding place.

The drive back home is bittersweet.

EIGHTEEN.

IT'S LATE IN the afternoon, and Naida and the day's hunting party have returned with the catch. But instead of joining the others in feasting on the fish, Linneth pulls Morgan aside.

"I know, I'm not going to go ashore," Morgan says flatly. "I will honor the terms of the Request and try not to see him again."

"I was wrong. If you want to see him, you should go see him to your heart's content and memorize what he looks like, before you forget. Today, of all days, I should not have kept you away from what you desire. If it is what you want—you should go see him. It is not against the rules so long as he doesn't see you."

Morgan gasps, hardly believing her change in mood. "What?"

"You have a few hours before you will need to return. Go on."

Morgan nuzzles against her quickly, and she harumphs fondly, pushing him toward the tide.

Morgan swims quickly, heart racing at the possibility of seeing Kevin again. The hour's travel passes quickly, and he soon arrives at the cove. He considers transforming and walking ashore, but that increases the chance of Kevin seeing him. Morgan doesn't want to incur the wrath of the Sea; this little town doesn't deserve a terrible storm because Morgan couldn't stay away.

Morgan thinks about where Kevin might be, and swims toward the pier where he met Kevin.

Sure enough, Kevin is sitting at the edge, watching the horizon with a melancholy look on his face. Morgan sighs happily, watching from the tide, but then realizes he'll be visible if Kevin is looking out to sea.

He isn't alone; a few fishermen stand off to the other side with their lines, waiting for a bite. Morgan dives and swims toward the pier, intending to watch Kevin from behind, and he swims past the fishing lines, taking care to avoid the hooks. But there are neither hooks nor bait at the end of these lines, only small weights to keep them in the water.

Something cold uncoils in Morgan's gut, and he resurfaces just in time to see the two fishermen leave their poles unattended and walk toward Kevin, then grab him roughly by the shoulders.

Morgan wants to transform, to scream in alarm, but that would mean revealing his presence to Kevin—but surely his safety is more important—

One of the men presses a small cloth to Kevin's mouth, and he struggles against their hold for a minute. Then Kevin's eyes close and he slumps forward.

Nineteen.

KEVIN WAKES WITH a pounding headache. He opens his eyes, trying to make sense of what is happening, but all he can see in front of him is the rough fabric of a canvas bag. Diffuse light filters through it, and Kevin can make out the logo from the local supermarket emblazoned on the white fabric.

He's sitting on a chair with his arms and legs bound tightly with rope. Kevin can hear the sound of waves in the distance, and people talking in agitated voices. He tries to keep calm, but every nerve in his body is electric with fear.

All he can remember is sitting on the pier, minding his own business, staring out at the horizon, watching the waves come in. And the fishermen. It isn't unusual for people to come to the pier to cast a line, and he nodded a greeting when they set up shortly after he arrived. Then he forgot about them, except for noting that one of them seemed familiar, maybe a tourist he'd seen earlier in the summer.

Kevin has no idea how long he was lost in his thoughts, watching the ocean. When he heard the footsteps behind him he turned to see what the men wanted, figured they might need an extra hand carrying a big fish, but then they were grabbing him by the arm and holding something over his mouth, and now Kevin is here.

He runs through everything he knows about kidnappings, thinks about what they might want from him, and tries to stay calm. He doesn't appear to be hurt, only immobilized. And while he has no idea how long he's been unconscious or where they've taken him, he can reason from what he does know.

The grocery bag is from Piedras Blancas. It's possible they're still close to town. They're near the shore, and Kevin can hear the sound of engines, maybe boats. Are they near the docks?

He tests the restraints, shifting and struggling, but they're knotted too tight.

"Boy's awake!" a rough male voice calls out.

Kevin blinks when the bag is removed from his head, and he tries to get a sense of his surroundings. They're in a boathouse. He can smell salt in the air, and that window looks out to the ocean and the lighthouse. His chair is right up against the center opening, where a small fishing boat is docked, bobbing in the current. Water occasionally splashes onto the wooden plank floor.

He sees three people: a man with too much gel in his slicked-back red hair, who holds the bag and stares at Kevin with an awed expression; an older man with a fierce scowl and crossed arms; and a young black woman, probably Sally's age, who is holding a notebook.

"We've got you," Hair Gel says, grinning at Kevin.

"Please," Kevin says, remembering a documentary about appealing to your captor's humanity. "I have parents and a sister, and friends... They'll miss me... Please let me call my parents. We have some money, please—"

"We're not interested in money." The older man in the corner steps forward, radiating confidence. Kevin straightens up, apprehensive. "We want to know where the rest of the selkies are."

Kevin knows where he's seen this man before, now: at the cafe, with these people, poring over maps. He thought they were hikers, and now, seeing the maps taped to the wall with charts of ocean currents, the photos of seals and drawings of potential transformations, a detailed drawing of a pelt, Kevin realizes these must be the people Morgan was talking about. Hunters.

Kevin's heart drops to his stomach. "I don't know what you're talking about."

On a far table he can see a number of metal instruments: medical instruments, scalpels and other things he has no name for, with sharp edges glinting in the low light. They must see the terror in his eyes, because the woman covers the table with a swath of fabric, glaring at the older man.

"I told you having those out would be overkill, Nathaniel," she says, shaking her head. "I thought you said this would be a quick questioning, not a torture session. He's just a kid."

"I'm sixteen," Kevin says, hoping to look as pathetic and non-threatening as possible.

"Won't the others come after him, if we've got him?" Hair Gel says.

"They're not like that; they'd cut their losses and save the rest of the herd," the old guy—Nathaniel—says, eyeing Kevin with interest.

They think I'm a selkie.

Nathaniel walks forward, and Kevin notices a gun on his hip. There's no doubt that he's the most dangerous of the group. Would they let him go let him go if he told them he's human? What if he's useless? How many action movies has he seen where they kill the witnesses to destroy evidence and tie up loose ends? Already Kevin has seen their faces, and knows what their hideout looks like.

They're probably planning to kill him anyway. Or dissect him, or worse.

The best he can do is not give up any information. He can't betray Morgan and Morgan's family.

"All right, selkie, where's the beach? I know it's around here somewhere, and I'm pretty sure none of you are staying at the rookery. It's funny, we've been here for awhile and we almost decided to move on, but then we saw you on the beach with that pelt and, well—" Nathaniel smiles, but the mirth doesn't quite reach his eyes. It makes him seem menacing, hungry.

"Where is the rest of the herd?" he asks again, pushing Hair Gel out of the way, leaning into Kevin's space.

"I don't know what you're talking about." Kevin spits at the man. Kevin understands science, understands being passionate about something and wanting to learn all about it, but to hurt another person deliberately—that's just cruel.

Nathaniel's face hardens, and he says, "You and your kind," right into Kevin's ear. Kevin can feel his hot breath, and it makes him bristle.

"You're scaring him," the woman says, and she pulls Nathaniel away. Kevin shoots her a grateful look, and she nods, the movement barely perceptible, but Kevin sees it. She seems to be the most sensible person in the room; maybe she'll convince the others to let Kevin go. She argues with Nathaniel, but just as Kevin is starting to hope, the man suddenly kicks his chair backward, causing Kevin to fall backwards into the opening.

The cold water is a shock, and Kevin sinks easily, weighed down by the chair. He struggles as the shimmering light of the surface becomes more and more distant. The chair pulls him toward the darker depths of the bay, and Kevin panics, using the last of his energy to thrash wildly. Water surges up his nose, and he's dizzy, but he has to try to get free somehow.

And then something hard collides with the back of his head, and it all goes dark again.

TWENTY.

"HE'S IN TROUBLE. Some people took him. I think it was the hunters. They were looking for selkies, for proof—and me. They took him, and it's my fault."

Morgan doesn't bother with a greeting when the cottage door opens, but he's gasping for breath, having run all the way from the pier. He transformed immediately, and Floyd was the only person he could think of to go to for help. He didn't return to the cave where his clothing was stashed, just ran straight here, his pelt under his arm.

Floyd doesn't say anything, just looks at Morgan carefully. There's a long silence, only broken by the sporadic drips of water from Morgan onto the stone step, and finally Morgan can't take it anymore, and pleads again. "Please. You told me you used to know them. Do you have any idea where they might be?"

FLOYD GIVES MORGAN a shirt and pair of shorts, grumbling about Morgan's nakedness despite Morgan's insistence that they need to leave.

"Ain't gonna take but a minute, kid. Woulda fed and clothed you all these years, but I couldn't, and now I can, so just let me."

Morgan gets dressed, feeling strange but appreciative as he tugs on the too-large shirt. The collar drapes awkwardly low on his neck, and the shorts don't stay up at all until Floyd finds him a piece of frayed rope.

"Eh, it's a work in progress," Floyd mutters. "Let's go get your boyfriend."

Floyd drags a dusty old cover off what Morgan thought was a huge pile of trash the first time he visited, but is actually an old pickup truck. It rumbles and spits when Floyd starts it, but it seems steady enough. Floyd buckles Morgan in carefully, and then they're off, down the bumpy dirt road that will connect them to the road leading into town.

Morgan grips his seatbelt in one hand and his pelt in the other as he listens to Floyd explain a bit more about this group as they drive. He had been one of these enthusiasts, convinced that the supernatural existed among them and was dangerous. There are a quite a few different factions scattered across the globe, focused on different types of "creatures." A chill goes down Morgan's spine as he hears the way Floyd talks about these people who used to be his friends, the sharp way they spoke of their goal to catch real, live proof that these creatures existed, and bring them to a facility for study.

"They're not going to hurt Kevin, are they?"

"He's a kid, like you. I don't think they have it in them. But we better hurry. I don't really know what they've been up to since I left."

A strangled, pitiful sob echoes through the truck, and Morgan realizes it came from him. Floyd gives him a tentative pat. "I'm sorry I don't have radio, otherwise I could put something on to relax you, or—"

"It's fine. How long will it take to get there?"

"'Bout fifteen minutes or so to the docks. This old thing can't go faster than thirty miles an hour, I'm sorry. It's the best I can do."

"Okay." Morgan takes a deep breath. "Just tell me a story or something."

"Not really a good storyteller, but I can try. Haven't led much of an interesting life—aside from my time with your mother, that is."

"Tell me how you met, then."

Floyd's smile is wistful, and for a moment he looks exactly like the man in the photo. "It was an accident. The best accident of my life, really."

As Morgan listens, the years seem to melt away from Floyd's face, revealing the man he once was. Listening to Floyd reminisce immediately takes Morgan's mind off his current stress.

"I was a student then, studying to get my PhD. I don't know if you know what that is, being a selkie and all—"

"Kevin's parents are both professors. I know what it is."

"Ah, yes, they're good people. I'd dropped out long before they started teaching at the school, but I've heard of their work. I don't really keep up with the research nowadays. I mostly just—" Floyd coughs, embarrassed.

"It's okay," Morgan says, surprising himself with how much he means it. "So you were studying?"

"Biology. Loved being outside, loved the idea of being in the field, ankle deep in some tide pool, figuring stuff out. Anyway, I'd run with Nate's group for a time, some romantic notion about the mysteries of the deep, learning more about the unknown. *Selkies.* They were convinced they were gonna find one, get published for discovering a new species. I thought it was incredible at the time, being part of this grand quest for knowledge." Floyd shakes his head. "I was such a fool. I didn't deserve her, and yet there she was."

He stops talking for such a long moment that Morgan is afraid Floyd's lost track of the story, or forgotten that Morgan is still in the truck with him. Finally Floyd blinks, drawn out of the memory, and continues, voice heavy. "I'd been kayaking out in the ocean through some rough waves, but I was young and rash; I thought I could handle it, was way too eager to get to my fishing spot. A wave knocked over my kayak, and I got tangled up and trapped in all my fishing gear. Couldn't get free from the kayak, thought I was gonna die, was blubbering about like it was my last, just wishing for some air."

It was a Request, Morgan realizes. If Floyd had been struggling with the Sea and crying, his heart's desire would have gone out, and the nearest selkie herd would have taken the call.

"Your mom, she—she dragged me out of there like I weighed nothing, pulled me to the shore and sat with me until I'd calmed down. I thought it was a dream at first, until she laughed at me, said I was the silliest human she'd ever met, and told me not to make a habit of putting myself in danger." Floyd chuckles. "I said I was in danger of a broken heart if she didn't go to dinner with me."

Floyd sighs, and the scent of happy memories is overpowered by the tang of guilt and sorrow. What it would it have been like, having him for a father? It's interesting, the way the real man is neither the harrowing villain Morgan's family has made him out to be, nor the dashing lost love he thinks his mother still imagines sometimes. Floyd's just a jaded fisherman who throws out an arm to brace Morgan when the truck brakes suddenly at a light, and looks at him across the console, full of regret.

"There's a boathouse by the docks that we used to use; I'm pretty sure Nathaniel still owns it. Saw their boat there a few times this summer," Floyd mutters as they pull into the parking lot by the docks.

"Which one is it?"

Floyd nods toward a boathouse in the distance with a big number "18" painted on its side.

"Thank you for your help," he says quickly, getting out of the truck. He's surprised when Floyd follows him toward the docks.

"What are you doing?"

"What are *you* doing? Do you have a plan?"

Morgan shakes his head. "Just going to try and see if I can get him out of there." He decides quickly that the best approach is from the water, and steps out of Floyd's clothes, handing them back to him. "Thank you for your help. For what it's worth, I think I would have liked you as a father." It's worth it to see Floyd's face light up.

Morgan nods at him, holds his pelt close and dives into the water, where he transforms quickly.

Floyd calls after him, "Good luck, kid! I'll be here if you need someone to punch that asshole in the face. Let me know!"

Morgan waves a flipper at him and dives. He swims quickly, heading toward the boathouse and listening for sounds of distress. He can smell excitement, fear and anxiety when he gets closer, and he swims into the entrance of the boathouse, grateful for the many shadows that disguise his head when he peeks out to see what is happening.

Kevin is bound to a chair, squirming ferociously as the hunters interrogate him.

"Where is the rest of the herd?"

"I don't know what you're talking about." Kevin spits at the leering man's face.

"You and your kind," he says, hissing in Kevin's ear. Morgan glares at him. It does no good; no one can see him. He hopes he can do something, anything, to get Kevin out of here. It's too late to swim for help, human or selkie or otherwise.

One of the hunters, a girl with dark skin and flyaway curly hair, shakes her head, grabs the man's arm and pulls him back. "You're scaring him," she says, scowling at him. "This isn't—this isn't what I signed up for."

"You wanted to see the world, Amanda. You told me you would give anything to see the magic out there. And here it is, in front of your face. It's not all rainbows and sunshine and unicorns, you know. To get answers you have to get your hands dirty."

The man shoves the chair, and Kevin's eyes widen as the chair tilts backward. Time seems to slow to a halt and Morgan has to bite his tongue on a cry of horror when Kevin falls with a loud splash.

The woman, Amanda, gasps. "He's tied to the chair, you moron! We can't—we have to get him! He doesn't have his pelt, either; he can't transform; you've as good as drowned him—"

The man seizes her around the waist before she can dive in after Kevin, and Morgan realizes these people aren't going to go after Kevin. He dives underwater, and can still hear the voice of the man talking coldly to his protesting colleague. "They have many abilities, even in human form. I'm sure he'll call one of his little friends to help him. You can observe, since you seem to like that so much."

The voices on the surface fade as Morgan tries to concentrate, adjusting to the murky light in the water. The water in the harbor is dark, filled with trash and other floating debris.

When Morgan spots Kevin his hair is floating above his head and his face is barely illuminated by the shafts of green light filtering through the water. Kevin struggles uselessly in his bonds, and then knocks himself into a boulder.

Morgan yells, but Kevin's name comes out as a strangled bark. Kevin won't be able to understand him as a seal. Morgan dives, watching helplessly as Kevin's eyes close and his limbs droop, all the fight gone out of him. No, no, he can't be—

Morgan can hear the Sea all around him, the magic ebbing and flowing, but he can't think of any question, any information he could possibly ask for right now, other than, "*Will he survive?*"

Morgan reaches Kevin, and he noses at Kevin's face, trying to free him from the ropes and the chair, but his flippers are useless. Morgan shifts quickly, not even thinking of securing his pelt around his shoulders or his waist, only of saving Kevin.

Kevin's heart is still beating, strong against his skin, but his eyes are closed and he doesn't—he needs, he needs—

Air.

Without thinking, he seals his lips to Kevin's in a kiss, breathing into him gently. It takes a moment, and then Kevin's chest rises and falls.

Morgan is heavy with relief. He undoes the knotted rope as quickly as he can, stopping to give Kevin the rest of the stored air in his lungs, and finally frees him. Morgan grabs Kevin under his arms and swims for the surface. He angles sharply to the right, away from the rest of the docks, and swims. His arms grow tired from Kevin's weight, but Morgan doesn't think about that and just keeps going.

They break the surface a good distance away from the docks. Morgan can't see the buildings, but they might still be in sight of the hunters. Kevin seems to be breathing on his own now that they're above the water, so Morgan takes care to keep his head aloft. It's difficult, holding Kevin and swimming at the same time, but Morgan presses on, even as his strength wanes.

They reach the cove where Kevin first took him to collect rocks, and Morgan drags Kevin gently to shore. His eyes flicker open, then shut, as Morgan lays him on the beach. "Morgan?" Kevin asks weakly, reaching for Morgan's face. "This is a dream…"

"Yes," Morgan says, letting Kevin touch him. He holds Kevin's hand against his cheek, closes his eyes and tries to memorize how this feels. It breaks his heart to see Kevin like this, and he knows he's breaking the rules by letting Kevin see him now. But at least Kevin thinks it's a dream.

"Good dream," Kevin says. His other hand is on the back of Morgan's neck, guiding him forward.

The kiss is short, and Kevin smiles, closing his eyes, his head falling back in fatigue. Morgan kisses him once more on the forehead; his heart swells with bittersweet longing. "I love you."

"Love you," Kevin whispers back, a small, fond smile on his lips.

Morgan lets go of Kevin's hand and steps back, wiping the tear threatening to fall down his cheek. He turns back to the surf and wades out into the water.

It would be faster to swim if he shifted back into a seal, Morgan realizes after a minute of paddling doggedly, exhausted. He concentrates, and then blinks in confusion.

His pelt. What did he do with his pelt?

* * *

MORGAN IS TOO tired to tread water for much longer, and a tingle of anxiety runs down his spine. He's never not known exactly where his pelt is at all times, other than that one harrowing day it went missing from the cave, but Kevin had it, and returned it promptly. No one else can connect the pelt to him, but there *are* a few people who might know what exactly it is.

Morgan is cold to the bone. He's closer to the docks, and thankful for the falling twilight so his nudity won't be obvious if he goes ashore. He could swim back to the cove where his clothes are, but he just left Kevin there. Maybe wait for an hour, go back, get dressed and comb the beach on foot?

There's only one boat out, and Morgan instinctively wants to dive to the bottom, but his current body needs a constant supply of air, so he settles for ducking lower in the water, hoping he's not visible.

He hears a familiar set of voices.

"You see anything?"

Someone surfaces in the water—Amanda, Morgan recognizes, now wearing a wetsuit and diving gear. "Give me a moment, okay. It's really dark down there. If that kid dies this is on you, Nathaniel, you know that, right?"

"Pssh, you bleeding-heart liberal. If you haven't found him by now, I'm sure he's gotten away. Wonder if Jake has that heat-tracking software up and running and found which way he's gone."

Amanda glares at him and dives back down.

Curiosity drives Morgan to take a deep breath and swim after her, to see what she's looking at. He follows the light from her headlamp, shining on the chair and pieces of ropes sitting silently on the ocean floor.

A bright rush of anger floods through him. They tried to hurt Kevin. Even if he were a selkie, he wouldn't have been able to transform without a pelt. Maybe he could have spoken to the Sea and asked for help, and another selkie could have heard, but that's…

That's exactly what they were hoping for. To lure someone else to capture, so they could have more people to study.

Morgan is so caught up in his thoughts that he doesn't see it until Amanda's light shines on the pelt caught in the rocks at the bottom of the harbor, swaying slightly in the drifting current. He darts forward, but it's too late, and it's already in her hands.

She stares at it incredulously, running a reverent hand over sleek fur, and starts to swim for the surface, not seeing Morgan in the dark shadows of the rocks.

He needs air, too; he can't forget that in this body.

Morgan surfaces a small distance from the boat, and hears them clamoring excitedly.

"Look, we have the pelt; we don't need the boy now. Just get Jake to run the tests, take a few samples and give it back to him," Amanda implores.

"No, that's not enough," Nathaniel says. "We need the boy *and* the pelt. I say we make up some fake gifted school, some excuse we can give his parents and get him to come with us. I still can't believe Mike's kid has been a selkie this whole time. Wonder if he got it from his mom. Always thought the boy was weird; he never shut up about the ocean and rocks."

"Take him away from his family?" Amanda gasps. "That's ridiculous."

"You have no idea how serious I am about this," Nathaniel says, a steely glint in his eye. "I've been made a mockery of in the scientific community ever since I suggested this species exists. I'm going to need living, breathing proof, not just another pelt that looks like it could come from any old seal."

Amanda clutches the pelt to her chest and shakes her head. "This has gone too far. I'm not your graduate student anymore. I only signed on to do this… *project* with you for the experience, and now I've got it, thanks. I'm gonna put this back where I found it."

Nathaniel sighs. "Fine. Do what you must."

Morgan feels a slim thread of relief as Amanda turns around to dive back in the water.

While she's putting on her diving mask, Nathaniel lunges for the pelt, pushing her roughly. Amanda screams as she topples over the side, and the pelt flies out of her hands. Nathaniel picks it up; his lips curve in a satisfied smile.

"Jake, take the boat back to the dock. We're gonna get ready to get this kid to come with us."

The boat engine whirrs, and starts speeding back toward the shore, and Amanda flails in the water.

Oh no.

They still think Kevin is the selkie.

"Don't touch him," Morgan says loudly, the strength of his voice startling himself. He swims toward the boat, past a startled Amanda, who treads water and stares at him incredulously.

The boat stalls, and Jake gapes at him as Morgan grabs the edge of the boat and peers aboard.

The two men stare at him, and Morgan glares with all the anger he can muster. "Leave him out of this. He's human. That—" and he jerks his head at the pelt in Nathaniel's hands— "that is mine."

Jake grabs for the pelt. "I want to see it, want to see him change."

"No! Give it back to him now and he'll swim away and all will be lost. Haven't you heard any of the stories? We have the pelt, we have all the power. He has to listen to us or he's stuck." Nathaniel grins, the white of his teeth blinding in the dark. He must have been a good-looking man, once, but Morgan doesn't have to ask the Sea what his intentions are, because he can see them from here—this man and his heart are terrifying.

"You're gonna take us to where the rest of you are, or we'll cut apart your pelt and you'll never get it back. And then I'll call up the rest of my team, and we'll have all the selkies at our disposal. Shifting cells? Body transmogrification? I'm gonna revolutionize the medical industry, prove I was right all those years ago when I first saw one of your kind." Nathaniel leers at him.

"No," Morgan says firmly. A part of him knows he's already lost, that his sealskin—the only thing that will let him return to the Sea— is already in the hands of people who mean him and his family harm.

"What do you mean, no? I've got your lifeline right here, and without it you're gonna sink, boy."

"I don't care. Do whatever you want with the pelt, but I'm not telling you where my family is. And you stay away from Kevin, too. He's no use to you."

Tears begin to well up in Morgan's eyes, and he's trembling with anger. He refuses to back down—to the hunters, to the traditions of his herd. Why does he have to choose? To live a paltry imitation of his former life just because of the Sea's ancient traditions about keeping the bloodlines separate? He can outright *refuse* to go either way— he doesn't have to only live in one world. This summer it's clear he's thrived on both land and sea; the need to separate the two seems trivial. The tears fall, but Morgan makes no move to wipe them away.

It doesn't matter anyway. Morgan is never going to make it back to his family's beach. They're never going to sing his name into the song celebrating the adults of their herd. He thinks of his mother watching Naida lead a song, watching her prepare for leadership; thinks about the pups rolling around in the sand without a care in the world; thinks of the young mated pairs like Micah and Oki, hopeful for the future; thinks of his entire herd, those he loved and grew up with— their safety and happiness is worth losing his freedom.

Morgan climbs onto the boat, standing steadily.

Nathaniel flips open a container and takes out a large, rusty pair of sharp scissors. "I'll cut it into pieces, I will," he says, sneering.

"Go ahead. I'm still not telling you."

Amanda has caught up with them, swimming up behind to Morgan. "Give it back to him, Nate," she calls out. "Cutting up his pelt won't do anyone any good. Leave the boy alone."

The scissors flash, and Morgan steels himself for the sensation of being separated irrevocably from the Sea. He wonders if after today he'll still lose his memory, stuck as a human.

"Boss, don't, look at this," Jake says, pulling the scissors away from Nate. He pushes a laptop at him. "I finally finished cleaning up the GPS data you had me stick on the kid's car for the past week. Looks like the boy took a trip up the coast yesterday. We've got the coordinates right here. We know where they are."

"We know where they are," Nathaniel repeats, eyes wide.

"No," Amanda gasps, next to him. "I am so sorry," she says, turning to Morgan. "I thought it was only going to be photos, or if we met any of you there would be questions, but I didn't think that he—"

"Take me instead," Morgan says, stepping forward. "Leave them alone. You can do your experiments on me. I'll go with you."

Amanda is climbing onto the boat next to him, and she hands him something—a large, hooded sweater that was on a bench. *Oh, right, I'm naked.* Morgan shrugs on the sweater, and it's so large it falls to his knees. He's tempted to pull the hood up and tighten the strings as he does with Kevin's sweater, but this isn't the time for comfort. He has to look strong.

"Really?" Nathaniel asks, raising his eyebrows.

"Yes."

"You don't have to do this," Amanda whispers. "It's a huge sacrifice, giving up your family, your ability to transform—"

"I'm protecting them. I do it gladly."

"Yes," Nathaniel quickly agrees.

Even though the sun just set, the sky is as dark as midnight. Clouds form above them in violent dark swirls and rain falls heavily, droplets hitting the boat's deck in a rapid *tat tat tat.* The humans on the boat yelp in confusion, and Morgan holds steady, watching it all. A large wave rushes toward them, flooding the boat. The others thrash about, searching for something to hold onto. The scene is utter chaos, but Morgan can sense the Sea whispering to him, and a calm settles in as the Sea flows all around him.

For a moment, he forgets he's on the boat. It's only him and the Sea, the endless centuries of magic and the ancient consciousness, and Morgan can feel the emotion—not of another selkie or someone else in the water, but of the Sea.

It's pride.

A pleased voice sounds in his head, and Morgan is so stunned he can't move. It's always been rather abstract, the way selkies have described "talking" to the Sea. Information comes and goes, and most people Morgan has talked to refer to it as an encyclopedia of sorts, a collective magic from which they pull stories or memories, and to which they add their own.

You did well, young halfling.

The voice—if Morgan could call it a voice—is like many voices speaking, layered over one another, in different languages, resonating powerfully.

I don't understand, Morgan responds.

It is a very old custom, choosing between worlds, and one that should have been retired long ago.

Everything changes, and the Sea is no different. The halflings that came before Morgan— and they were few and far between, he barely counts five different stories the Sea shows him—had little desire to see the human world, all but one deciding to stay with their herd. The other, the Sea only saw once more at the end of her life, and it had been a good one. She'd lived as a human for the rest of her years, with an unknowing pull to return to the Sea, and only accomplished that in her old age.

The Sea shows Morgan all of this in an instant, and then says, *The usual rule is seven years, to see the maker of a Request again—but I suppose seven months should be fine. Fare well, Morgan.*

And with that, the waves recede, and the clouds part. It's a soft purple twilight again, and the ocean is calm, as if the sudden storm never happened.

Nathaniel splutters, shaking himself. "What the hell was that?"

Morgan shrugs, smiling, feeling lighter than he has in a long time.

"The damn laptop got soaked. Jake, please tell me you backed that information up," he says, shaking the other man.

Jake frowns, and pushes his hair back. It doesn't look all that different wet than it did when it was gelled. "I was gonna do that once we got back to shore."

Amanda picks something off the deck of the boat—Morgan's pelt—and hands it to him. "I believe this is yours."

"You! You're fired!" Nathaniel hisses, pointing an accusing finger at her.

"You don't pay me." Amanda folds her arms and taps her foot on the deck.

Morgan holds his pelt hesitantly, not sure if this will work. It feels the same, the same current of potential energy hums under his fingertips.

"Go on, get out of here," Amanda says, nudging him forward.

Morgan jumps off the boat, the discarded sweatshirt floats away, and he swirls the pelt around himself, laughing in surprise when the transformation takes hold.

He dives gleefully and resurfaces, splashing.

Amanda jumps in the water with him, scuba gear all askew, watching him with spellbound eyes. Even Nathaniel and Jake are peering over the boat, gasping.

"You," Nathaniel says, pointing a finger at Jake. "Where's the camera, why aren't you recording this? We should be getting all this down, at least photos, something!" When Jake doesn't move, Nathaniel raises his voice, loud and shrill in the otherwise calm night. "You can't do this! I've worked so hard for this!" Nathaniel shouts, and at that Amanda gives an affected look, and Morgan gets the idea that she's done most of the work. "This was going to be my opus! I need to get my name back, and the scientific community will regret ever laughing—"

A sudden wave out of nowhere knocks the boat, and Nathaniel falls into the water, spluttering helplessly.

Jake looks from the man in the water to Amanda and Morgan, shrugs, and turns the boat back toward shore, the engine *putt-putt*ing rhythmically as Nathaniel yelps and paddles after him.

Morgan laughs again, and it comes out as a happy little bark. He is about to swim away when he sees Amanda wave goodbye to him.

The Sea finds the information easily: Amanda Everhart, age twenty-four, a graduate student in marine biology, who was trying to publish her work on seal community migration when her advisor, Nathaniel, enlisted her help with his wild goose chase. She is relieved that Morgan is free, and that Nathaniel doesn't have the selkie herd's location, but disheartened to have spent so much time away from her own thesis. She's crying happy, exhausted tears, but wishes she didn't have to go back to school alone, tail between her legs, without an advisor and with miles and miles of fieldwork to make up.

Morgan thinks about swimming back to the beach, where he knows everyone is getting ready to swim south. They'll follow the current, ending up on a bright beach where they can enjoy the sun and catch more fish and sing more songs. It'll be the same, every day.

He loves his family, but now that it's not forever, now that he doesn't have to choose—he'd gladly welcome the opportunity to see more of the human world. His older brothers and sisters have all spent copious amounts of time on land. Why not he?

And he has seven months before he can see Kevin again. Why not spend it doing something worthwhile?

Morgan nudges Amanda playfully, and she pats him on the head, smiles at him and wipes her face. Morgan tries to let her know everything is going to be okay, but realizes she can't understand him when he's a seal. He transforms and watches the boat trundle back to the docks with her.

Amanda shakes her head. "Good riddance."

"Hey," Morgan says. "Thank you for your help."

"It was nothing."

"The only reason I would come back to this town is for someone I'm not supposed to see for seven months." Morgan waves his hand vaguely in the air. "It's a magic thing. Anyway, I'd like to help you with your research. I mean, I do know a lot about currents."

"How do you know about my thesis—"

Morgan shrugs again. "The Sea knows your heart's intentions."

"And what about you? Don't you want to go home?"

Morgan looks at the shore, where the lights of the town are blinking awake, and then back at the horizon. "My home is wherever I am. I can see my family whenever I want. I don't have to choose anymore."

Amanda scrunches her nose, and Morgan chuckles. "It's a long story."

Twenty-one.

KEVIN WAKES UP, for the third time today, and with a head-ache. He's on the beach where he and Morgan collected rocks on that first hike so long ago. He sits up groggily, brushing sand off himself, trying to remember what happened. That Nathaniel guy pushed him into the water—to what—to see if he would transform? No, to see if he could call another selkie for help.

How did he end up all the way over here?

Kevin has a vague vision of Morgan holding him, and kissing him, telling him he loved him, but it slips away easily, as dreams do.

His head hurts, and Kevin recalls hitting it on a rock or some-thing. Did the chair break, then, if he hit the rocks on the ocean floor? Kevin recalls moving upward. He swam? Did he make it to the surface and then the tide washed him ashore?

He stands up wearily, rubbing his head; his wet clothes hang heavily on his body. It's going to be dark soon.

HIS PARENTS LOOK at him carefully, as if he's fragile and might break, and Kevin doesn't tell them about the kidnapping and the near-fatal incident. They'd only worry. He trudges up to his room on autopilot and takes a shower, barely going through the motions. He gets dressed, and stares at his reflection in the mirror. It all seems so pointless. Eventually he flops on his bed.

Kevin ignores the calls for dinner, and stares at the ceiling. He falls asleep, but it's an uneasy, restless sleep. He dreams he's in the water, struggling in the dark. Morgan is pulling him to the surface, laying him on the shore, kissing him once more before returning to the waves.

The next morning, Kevin gets up early. Ann's downstairs, stretching as she prepares to go for her morning run.

"Hey, loser," she says. "Funny seeing you up."

"Want some company?"

"Sure."

They jog to the shore and run up and down the beach. Kevin keeps up with Ann, even though he remembers her being faster. Maybe he's gotten fitter.

"You missed out on dumplings last night," Ann says on their third back-and-forth on the shore. "Dad and Rachel made them together as usual, and she made all the funny-looking ones. Not that they taste any different when they're cooked, but it was pretty hilarious, because the stuffing kept falling out of the ones she made."

Kevin nods and lets Ann make idle conversation, and they run, their breath forming small clouds in the early morning chill. Kevin gets tired after losing track of how many times they've been up and down the beach, and Ann takes pity on him, walking back with him toward the house.

"So you guys broke up, eh?" Ann says, quirking an eyebrow.

"I guess. I mean, I knew he was only visiting for the summer… I just forgot it was ending."

"It happens. You get so caught up in being happy, you lose sight of what's coming ahead."

Kevin sighs and keeps walking.

"You took my car somewhere yesterday," she adds.

"Sorry. I really, really needed to be alone. I went out for a hike on a beach Morgan took me to before, and I just… wanted to be there, I guess."

"It's fine, I'm not mad. I get it, you know. First real boyfriend, and now he's gone. Distance sucks. I'm guessing they don't have Wi-Fi on his parents' boat?"

"What? Boat, yeah. No, they won't have Wi-Fi. Or phones. They're, like, not a very technology-happy family."

"I could tell, the way Morgan was so fascinated with all your stuff. But especially you. He adored you, you know."

Kevin sighs.

"Sorry, I'm just trying to be helpful. Look, you know I don't start classes for a few weeks. You're welcome to take the car out for a drive whenever you want, okay? Heartbreak sucks; I've been there."

"Thanks, Ann, you're the best."

They walk along the last stretch of beach before hitting the road that leads to town and pass the lifeguard tower. Sally waves at them enthusiastically. "That looked like quite the workout!"

"Thanks," Kevin says. "It's way too intense for me, though. Can't believe Ann does this every day."

"I know," Sally replies, lifting her eyebrows at Ann.

To Kevin's great surprise, Ann blushes, grabs Kevin by the arm and then quickens their pace. "Kaythanksbye," Ann mumbles, leading Kevin away.

"Whaaaat was that?" Kevin teases as soon as they're out of earshot.

"What was what? That was nothing," Ann says, but the blush is deepening, traveling down her cheeks in full force.

"She was totally asking about you all summer. I didn't know you were—"

"I don't know if I am." Ann casts a wistful look back at the beach. "I mean, I never thought about it, actually, until you came out to us. I didn't even think bisexuality was a thing. I don't know if I ever told you how brave you were, when you told Dad and Rachel, you know? I know I wasn't home when all that shit went down in your school with that kid and stuff—"

"You were at college," Kevin points out. "It's not like you could have come back and done anything about that asshole."

"You're right, but I was really just wrapped up in my own life, and I kind of just took for granted what you were going through here. And then this summer while I've been at home, it's just been amazing to see you really happy, you know. I'm glad you're my brother."

"Ann," Kevin says shakily, overcome with affection for his sister.

She pulls him into a hug, even though Kevin knows she doesn't particularly like physical affection, and Kevin pats her back appreciatively.

KEVIN TAKES ANN up on her offer that afternoon, driving up the coast back toward the beach. He doesn't know if this is a good idea or not, but he wants to see Morgan again. Maybe from a distance, just to see if he's okay. He parks the car on the shoulder, steps out into the wind and finds the same hidden path through the chaparral.

Kevin makes his way to the shore, crouching down to stay out of sight, and the salty air whistles by; the smell of sage is heavy in the air. He peeps through the shrubbery, and then stands up in confusion.

The beach is empty.

There is no one, not in seal form or human form. It's strange, reconciling this bleak and empty shore with the busy one filled with laughter, seals wobbling around, toddlers running naked in the surf, pelts drying on the rocks.

Kevin walks out onto the sand, which is freshly wet from the receding tide. There's no trace of anyone ever having been here at all.

The entire summer could have been a dream.

He sits on the beach, waiting for the tide to change, watching the clouds run by.

It isn't until his phone chirps with a text message from Michelle, reminding him about lifeguard training, that he shakes himself out of his stupor.

Kevin takes a deep breath, watching the ocean. *It'll be fine.*

* * *

LIFE INVARIABLY DOES go on. Sometimes thoughts of Morgan surface at the oddest times, such as when his mom brings dinner home one day from the cafe, and he's taking French fries out of the bag. Or when Kevin's rearranging his rock collection and turns over the piece Morgan gave him. The hurt is familiar now, a deep ache that Kevin accepts he's going to have for a long time. He pushes the feeling deep down, focusing on keeping busy. Lifeguard training takes up most of his time before school starts. And then it's back into the routine, getting on the bus every day to go to Cambria.

Kevin sits with Michelle, Patrick and Connor in the back row, now that they're friends. Somehow he's never noticed, despite having gone to school with them for years, but they say they've claimed this row forever, and eagerly welcome Kevin. The bus rides don't seem so lonely anymore. Sometimes he sees Miles at school or on the bus, hanging out with his new soccer friends, and Miles always looks apprehensive, as if he's waiting for Kevin to out him.

Kevin ignores him.

He throws himself into his schoolwork, and takes up Ms. Tran's suggestion that he join the school newspaper staff. Michelle is a copy editor, and pleased to have another writer on board. Kevin's afternoons are filled with frantic work to meet deadlines, with fast food runs and with the collective energy of all the other students on the staff. It's fun; some of the kids he never bothered talking to in his first two years of high school are actually really nice.

"You know, I tried to eat lunch with you once," Michelle says, stealing a dumpling out of the lunch his dad packed for him.

Connor spears a dumpling as well, rooting around in the lunchbox with his other hand and grinning triumphantly when he finds the small container of sauce to go with it.

Patrick laughs at both of them, and pushes his plate of chicken nuggets and French fries toward Kevin. "Yeah, I remember. You said us Bus C kids should stick together, but this one just mumbled hello and kept reading his book."

"I didn't know you wanted to be friends! I was super paranoid at the time, okay? You don't remember what it was like," Kevin protests.

Patrick nudges a container of ketchup at him. "I think a lot of us thought you were very brave. I don't know if anyone else would have responded to Skylar's taunts with a 'YEAH I AM, SO WHAT?' and then head butted him."

Kevin shakes his head. "I ended up in the principal's office."

"It was pretty awesome," Patrick recalls. Kevin snorts at him and eats the offered chicken nuggets, and then starts to pick at Michelle's tater tots. "I think you were just trying really hard to play off the mysterious, bad-boy bisexual thing."

Kevin blushes. "I don't know what you were talking about. I was a loser."

Connor pulls a pastrami sandwich from his backpack and shakes it at Kevin. "And then you started hanging out with that Miles kid, and only him. I don't think anyone ever figured it out. Were you guys dating or something? Patrick was pretty devastated; he thought you were."

"Shut up," Patrick says hotly, nudging Connor. "And then this year, instead of hanging out with you, it looks like Miles signed up for Team Homophobes," he says, glancing at where the soccer team is eating lunch a few tables away.

"I, um, well, we were friends." Kevin has a brief impulse to tell them what happened, that he and Miles had been hooking up and then Miles had gone and pretended it was nothing. He could laugh with them about how Miles was in the closet or something, but it only seems cruel now. And pointless. "I guess we were close because we were neighbors, so I ended up hanging out with him a lot. I didn't think he was like that, but I guess when he joined the soccer team he decided not to be friends with me anymore."

Michelle pats Kevin on the shoulder. "His loss. Besides, you have us now."

Connor hands Kevin half of his pastrami sandwich, stuffed with all the sauerkraut that Kevin likes but Connor doesn't, and the four of them eat companionably, sharing their food, while Patrick tries to remember what exactly was on Ms. Tran's exam when he took AP US History last year as a junior.

They don't talk about Morgan. Michelle asked, on the first day, if Morgan would be at their high school, but Kevin just shook his head and said he moved away, and his friends seemed to take it upon themselves to not bring it up. Kevin talked about Morgan once with Patrick, when they were studying for their history class in Kevin's bedroom, and it had seemed so strangely reminiscent of the days spent with Morgan that Kevin had just stared off into the distance until Patrick asked about it. Kevin talked for an hour, skimming off the supernatural aspects of the story, and Patrick put his pen down and listened intently.

"It sounds like he was a great guy," Patrick said. And that was it: no judgment, no pitying "it's going to get better" remarks, just a simple affirmation of Kevin's feelings, and the invitation to talk more, if he wanted.

"He is," Kevin said, correcting the tense to the present.

Morgan still is, somewhere, a great guy.

Twenty-Two

MORGAN HAS A stomachache. He groans helplessly, leaning against the hard plastic seat of the diner.

"I told you not to get the fried platter," Amanda says, snickering. "A year later, you're still stuffing yourself sick."

Morgan holds his stomach. "It looked so good in the picture. And I like fried things."

"Mmhm, you're lucky you're a teenager; at a certain point all of that goes straight to your hips. Damn, you ate all of that." Amanda looks at the empty plates. Morgan finished the entirety of the fried seafood platter—fish and chips, fried oysters and a mound of fried shrimp. Two empty glasses that once held milkshakes round out the tableau.

"He's a growing boy," Floyd says proudly. "Did you want dessert? This place does cake, too." He pushes the menu at Morgan, smiling. His beard is a little scraggly since they've been camping for the past few days, but it's still a lot neater than it was when Morgan first met him. Floyd's eyes dance in amusement as he scans the menu. "What about the cheesecake sampler? Look, you can try all three flavors."

"Don't encourage him; I just got the check!" Amanda scoffs. "You're supposed to be setting a good example!"

Morgan laughs and puts the menu back in its little holder. "I don't think I can even look at dessert right now."

Amanda shakes her head fondly. "All right kiddo, sounds like a plan. Let's hit the road. Old man, you're not driving; the way you handle turns scares me senseless." She throws a generous tip onto the table and they head out of the diner; the bell tinkles merrily as they leave.

Morgan throws the hood of his sweatshirt over his head, and his father shakes his head at the worn and frayed old thing. "I bought you that other sweater; how come you never wear it?"

"This one was a gift," Morgan says, pulling on the strings so the hood tightens around his face. He takes a deep breath of the fabric. It's been a long time, so it may be mostly his imagination, thinking the sweatshirt still smells like Kevin.

Floyd pats him gently on the shoulder and gives him an understanding look.

Amanda has already started her hatchback's engine, and she has a map propped up on the steering wheel. "All right, so we head up to Vancouver and do some quick measurements up there, plus we can hit up my post office box, and by the time we get back to the university my satellite images should have arrived and I can do the thermal analysis. This time, Floyd, be careful with the instruments; I don't want to almost lose one to the tide. We're not always going to have no one around to see Morgan transform and get it for us."

"You're the boss," Floyd says.

Morgan sighs happily, curling in the backseat. The car's stuffed full of luggage, camping gear, an ice chest and Amanda's equipment, as well as her laptop and quite a few books. He wraps his arm around the pillow that has his sealskin tucked inside. He can smell the faintest hint of the sea as he smushes his face into it and watches the lights of the cars passing them by on the highway.

Amanda and Floyd argue companionably about music, and Floyd suggests taking some time to catch some fish. Morgan drifts off, watching the mountains in the dark distance, reading signs as they pass by.

They're in Vancouver when he wakes up, and Amanda is walking back to the car, shuffling through her mail. Morgan steps out of the car to stretch his legs and smells the salt in the air and the ocean nearby.

"Oh! Morgan, these are for you," she says, handing him a fat envelope.

Morgan looks through the contents quickly; a flare of warmth travels through his body. He has official identification now: he can register in high school and even… apply to college? He's been doing all right; Floyd and Amanda have been tutoring him while they're on the road doing her fieldwork, and Morgan knows from his time studying for the SAT with Kevin that the subject matters aren't that difficult.

Floyd ruffles Morgan's hair. "It's official."

Morgan looks at the California identification card—not a driver's license, although it certainly looks like one. He turns over the plastic in his hands and marvels at the shiny holograms. He has a place here now, and what he was worried about before—not being able to have a future—all of that is taken care of.

"Morgan Linneth Floyd," he reads, looking up at Floyd. "You gave me my mom's name, too."

"Amanda said the rhythm was off," Floyd shrugs. "I know you said it would be fine if it was just my name, but I wanted you to have both."

"Thank you." Morgan leaps forward and hugs him around the waist. They've spent a lot of time together on the road, and there were times when getting to know him was difficult. They argue sometimes, and Floyd doesn't understand when Morgan refuses his request to ask his mother to come see him, but he tries. They've been getting along a lot better, lately.

They collect data in Vancouver and a few more spots along the coast on their way to Amanda's university in Humboldt. There she'll be settling down, finishing her doctorate with a new group of supportive academic advisors, all eager to see the research she's been doing this year.

Morgan knows it's well past the seven-month mark, but when March came he was nervous about seeing Kevin again. What if Kevin has moved on? If he's forgotten about Morgan? If he's fallen in love with someone else? Morgan spent a lot of time thinking about it. He knows he only wants Kevin to be happy, and he thinks he'd be sad for himself, but it would be fine, eventually. Kevin deserves to be happy, whether it's with Morgan or not.

He considered leaving, when it was exactly seven months since he left Piedras Blancas, but it would have meant stranding Amanda without two valuable research assistants, and he didn't have the heart to do that, especially when she designed a new line of investigation based on what Morgan was able to find for her in seal form. Plus, the research was interesting, and he adored Amanda, and there was no way of knowing if Kevin still felt the same way about him. And then Amanda wanted to do some studies on the Aleutian Current, and that was a seasonal investigation, and Floyd had never been to Alaska, and it was just easy to keep going along with their current plan instead of facing the possibility that Kevin might not want him anymore.

"You all right, son?" Floyd asks, joining him on the cliff's edge where he's looking across the sea. This particular stretch of Oregon coast is lonely and rocky, and rather desolate, and Morgan is filled with a sudden pang of longing for the sounds and laughter of his herd around him, for Naida gently teasing him about something or other, even for Micah's smug face.

"Yeah, just thinking."

Floyd sits down next to him, and they spend a few companionable moments watching the waves together. It's been nice, getting to know him. He has a dry sense of humor and a sharp way of looking at the world that Morgan appreciates. Morgan felt guilty at first, as if getting to know Floyd would be disloyal to Joren, his mother's current mate, who helped raise him since he was a pup. But now he knows he doesn't love Joren any less by learning to love Floyd.

His father nudges him. "Those look like seals, you think? Cousins of yours?"

Morgan sees the dark shapes in the distance and smiles. "Sure."

"What are they saying?"

Morgan can't hear the barks well enough to translate. "I don't know if it will be very interesting, even if I could understand them," he says, laughing. "We're not exactly the same."

Floyd laughs, and they watch the seals together.

One of them swims forward, and Morgan recognizes the silhouette. Warmth rushes through him, and he wants to find the trail and race down to the shoreline to say hello, but then remembers he isn't alone.

"I'll be right back," Morgan says.

"Oh, one of them is a selkie?"

"I'll only be a moment." Morgan hesitates, wondering if he should tell—no, it isn't his decision to make.

Floyd waves him off as Morgan runs down the trail, picking his way through the sharp turns that go down the cliffside. He's panting when he gets to the beach.

"Mother!" Morgan calls out.

She transforms and smiles warmly at Morgan, but doesn't walk ashore yet, just stands there in the surf as another wave breaks around her. Morgan follows her gaze up toward the cliff.

Toward his father.

Linneth and Floyd look at each other, and every second seems to stretch out like the years they've been apart, as if they're thinking about the time they had together, the decisions that were made, the would-haves and should-haves and where they are now. Finally Linneth waves, gives Floyd a soft smile. There's a lot said with that single look—love, thankfulness and appreciation.

Morgan smiles and waits on the beach, watching his parents have this moment to say hello. And goodbye.

FLOYD'S TRUCK IS parked in the lot of Amanda's new apartment in Humboldt, and they start unloading Amanda's car, separating their belongings.

"Thank you so much for your help this year," Amanda says, sweeping them both up in hugs. "I really couldn't have done it without you."

"Thank you for taking us along," Morgan says. Amanda's personality reminds him of Naida, a little bit, and he looks up to her with the same fondness with which he regards his siblings. "I'll miss you."

"Where are you guys going now?" Amanda asks. "Gonna go check out some redwoods maybe? Or go east? Lots of cool stuff out there, you know."

"Home," Morgan says, without hesitation.

Twenty-Three

THE MORNING IS gray on Kevin's first day of senior year. He smiles at the cloudy sky as he laces his shoes for his daily run. The chilly ocean air whips past him as he jogs down the beach, and Kevin sprints past the closed lifeguard tower, checking his watch as he goes. He considers taking the extra time to run down the pier and back, and thinks he'll still have time to do his usual route, get home, shower and catch the bus to school.

Kevin jogs down the pier, his feet making satisfying *clunks* against the wood that stand out from the crashing of the waves into the pillars below. The ocean churns on endlessly, and Kevin smiles, thinking about the picture he makes, a lone figure in the middle of all of it. He's humbled and awed, grateful for his place in the vast universe.

He takes a moment to pause at the end of the pier, standing there to watch the waves come in.

There's a seal in the water.

It's too far out for Kevin to see it clearly, but he knows in his heart it's a seal.

Kevin waves at it, laughing. "Welcome to Piedras Blancas!"
And then there's no time to linger. He's got to get to school.

"LOOKING GOOD, LUONG!"

"Thanks." Kevin smiles. He doesn't remember what the freshman's name is, but they're on the swim team together.

The guy blushes and Kevin can hear him and his friends giggling as he continues down the hallway. Kevin shakes his head, still in disbelief that some people find him cool. He had a growth spurt his junior year, and shot up a few inches. Michelle's still peeved she's not the tallest one in their group of friends anymore. It's still hilarious to Kevin. He turns down another hallway.

He passes Skylar, who narrows his eyes at Kevin, but doesn't say anything, just starts walking in the other direction. Skylar's without his usual group of hangers-on, which has something to do with his less-than-stellar performance on the soccer team last year. Kevin stopped caring about Skylar and his annoying little homophobic group of friends, spent the whole junior year ignoring them. He spent his lunchtimes either with his friends or his favorite English teacher and the rest of the student newspaper staff, instead of eating in the cafeteria and hoping to avoid getting picked on.

The new swim team trophy looks great in that display case. Kevin smiles at it fondly, as if he's greeting an old friend, remembering the state championships last year. Patrick laughed at him and said Kevin cheated, because he joined the swim team when Patrick was promoted to team captain, and clearly it was Patrick's leadership that guided them to victory. Maybe it was, or maybe it was Kevin's backstroke. The jury's still out on that one.

Yeah, last year was a good year. Being involved in activities outside of class also meant his time was quickly filled with staying late after school for newspaper deadlines, cracking jokes in the pool with the other swimmers and late night team dinners after swim meets, and somehow Kevin went from being a loner to having friends. He got great SAT scores and already had a lot of ideas for his college applications.

He'd even dated a little, with the encouragement of his friends. Kevin took Jennifer, the opinions editor from the *Gazette,* out to the movies once, and he was definitely attracted to her, but couldn't seem to get into the headspace of dating again.

"I'm sorry, I really like you, I'm just—"

"Still in love with your ex?" Jennifer asked.

"Yeah." It didn't hurt anymore, but he wasn't quite ready to date again.

Jennifer had laughed good-naturedly and appreciated his honesty, and they went to Homecoming as friends.

Kevin waves at Michelle and Connor, not that they'll notice him, the way they're making out by Connor's locker. Kevin shakes his head in fond mock-annoyance as he walks by his friends. Whistling, he finds his locker. Who would have thought: Senior year is here and Kevin has nothing but confidence. It's going to be a good year.

Someone taps him on the shoulder and Kevin turns around. Miles is standing behind him, looking a little nervous and sheepish. "Hey, Kevin," he says awkwardly, shifting on his feet. Miles runs his hand through his hair, the way Kevin used to think was so *hot,* but it looks pointlessly pretentious now.

"Miles," Kevin says, deadpan. For all that they're neighbors, they haven't spoken to each other since, well. Kevin doesn't really care anymore. Hasn't cared for a long time, and doesn't ever want to be used like that again.

"So I was thinking, you know, since Patrick graduated and I hear you're gonna be the new swim captain, which I think is cool and major congrats by the way, it's just a shame we fell out of touch, y'know. We used to be such good friends—"

"No." Kevin finds the textbook he needs for first period, shuts the locker with a definite slam, walks right past Miles and doesn't look back.

A few kids from drama whistle, and one of them says, "Sick burn, dude," offering his fist for Kevin to bump. Kevin taps it with a small smile and keeps going down the hallway.

A girl walks past him with a purse patterned with seals, and Kevin blinks. He thinks about the seal he saw this morning; memories flicker through his mind. It's been over a year, and he's proud of himself for not having tried to find the selkies' hidden beach again this summer. Kevin spent all of this summer as a junior lifeguard under Sally's mentorship, working every day at the beach. It was fun; he got a bit tanner, and worked hard to maintain the fitness he needed in order to be a lifeguard. He still misses Morgan, but he isn't sad when he thinks about him anymore; the first few weeks after Morgan left even the mention of the sea had caused Kevin anguish.

Today he smiles, remembering Morgan's bright laugh.

Kevin shakes himself; the memory is so clear it's almost as if he's hearing it.

"Hello, Kevin," a familiar voice sounds behind him.

Kevin whirls around so fast he nearly falls over, and he can hardly believe it. Morgan is standing there, grinning widely, face shining like the sun. He's actually wearing clothes—T-shirt, jeans, shoes and Kevin's sweatshirt.

"Morgan." Kevin gasps, voice barely a whisper, as though he's afraid to break the illusion. "How...?"

Morgan shrugs. "The Sea is ancient and deep, full of secrets. Besides, selkies can cry, too, you know."

"Morgan," Kevin says, still awed. "You're really here. To stay?"

Morgan just says, "I love you," as if it's the simplest thing in the world to him, and it is.

Kevin stares for what seems like an eternity, as if he's daring himself to wake up and realize this is a dream.

It's real.

Morgan is standing here in front of him, and students mill about in the hallway on their way to class, talking and laughing, but everything seems to be muted except for Morgan's smile.

The smile falters, and Kevin realizes he's been staring, and he needs to will his body to start working again, his mind to think, respond—

"I love you." The words are easy, like a song he knows by heart.

Morgan steps forward, and Kevin can't help but sweep him into his arms and kiss him; his body is overflowing with warmth and happiness as Morgan kisses back with equal enthusiasm.

Kevin would keep kissing Morgan forever, but the warning bell is ringing, and there are a few wolf whistles from behind them. Kevin lets Morgan go reluctantly. He can't help the ridiculous smile he knows is on his face. He pulls Morgan into the nearest classroom and checks to make sure it's empty, and yes, this is the chemistry lab; no one will use this until second period. As soon as the door is closed, he reaches for Morgan again, taking the time to reverently cup his face in his hands. Morgan sighs in appreciation and kisses him slowly, as if he's breathing him in, and Kevin follows his lead, holding him close as if he's been adrift at sea forever and now he's finally found his anchor.

It's forever, and still not enough, by the time the bell rings again. Kevin pulls away reluctantly, still dazed, and Morgan looks overwhelmed as well. He's just as lovely as Kevin remembers him; his skin is flushed from the slight exertion and his lips are kiss-swollen. Kevin wants to kiss him again, hear him make that noise again.

"I thought you might have—you might have forgotten me," Morgan says breathlessly.

"Never."

The bell stops ringing. Kevin's really late now, but he doesn't care.

"We should get to class," Morgan murmurs, even as he takes Kevin's hand and interlaces their fingers.

"We?"

Morgan grins at him, eyes bright with mischief. He swings his backpack around—an actual backpack that he's digging in with his other hand, pulling out a sheet of paper to show to Kevin. "My class schedule."

"Really?"

"Where's yours? I want to see if we've got anything in common."

Kevin pulls the sheet out of a notebook in his own backpack, amazed as Morgan hums to himself, comparing the two schedules. Morgan's a little taller, and his speech pattern seems a more relaxed, but he's still the same, adorable freckles and all. And is that the tune of "Somewhere Beyond The Sea" he's humming? Morgan looks up and sees Kevin staring at him, and he winks—actually winks at him. When did this boy get so cheeky?

"Mmhm, looks like we've got four classes together. Is there any way I could change my last class to yours?" Kevin sees Morgan pointing at where his own schedule says "GYM" and Kevin's says "SWIM TEAM."

"Yeah, you could. You'd have to try out, though," Kevin says. He pinches himself to make sure this isn't all a dream, and the pinch stings, so he's definitely awake.

Morgan scrunches up his face. "You think I'd be any good?".

Kevin stares at him before Morgan bursts out laughing, and Kevin has to kiss him again to make sure he's real.

"You gonna tell me how this all works, you being here? And you're… staying?" Kevin asks as they step into the empty hallway. Part of him is worried there's another catch to this, as though Morgan will stay only for the fall quarter, but Morgan smiles at him again as if he knows exactly what he's thinking.

"Yes, I'm staying. And I can tell you all about it, you know, after class. I gotta keep my grades up. College applications and all that."

He looks knowingly at Kevin, and Kevin blinks a little in surprise, the weight of it settling in. Morgan is staying. He's going to be here for Kevin's senior year—he's applying to *colleges*. There's an unwritten future stretched out in Kevin's imagination, and where he's always pictured himself alone before, now he can see Morgan there with him.

The classroom is rowdy, full of students eagerly catching up on each other's summers. Luckily Ms. Tran hasn't arrived yet to mark anyone tardy. Kevin is still thinking about it as he plops down in an empty seat. Morgan takes the seat in front of him, looking incredibly at home at a classroom desk. Wearing sneakers, of all things. Even their laces are tied properly in neat little bows.

Morgan's eyes are sparkling when he turns around. "Hi."

"Hello."

Morgan kisses him again, and Kevin forgets he's in the middle of a classroom filled with his peers—some of whom make whooping noises.

He only comes back to reality when he hears a sharp rapping on a desk and sees Ms. Tran looking disapprovingly at them. She glares at everyone in the classroom, trying to get them to calm down. "Mr. Luong! And… you, new student. No public displays of affection, please."

Kevin grins sheepishly. "Sorry, my boyfriend moved back to town, and I'm just really excited."

Morgan shrugs, turns around to look back up at their teacher with an innocent face.

He does slip his hand back under Kevin's desk, though, and Kevin takes it and squeezes. He's still curious, and can't wrap his head around what kind of magic would let Morgan come back. While Ms. Tran is busy passing out syllabi, Kevin leans forward and whispers, "How?"

Morgan turns around to look at him, whispering in turn, "We have all the time in the world, to talk, to do anything we want." He squeezes Kevin's hand, and Kevin relaxes a little.

Yeah, they do.

THE END

Acknowledgments

THERE ARE SCORES of people I would love to thank, and if I had the luxury to do so I would love to fill another book with the names of everyone who's ever believed in me.

For my parents, the hard lives you have had, surviving war and famine and constant fear, your endeavors for freedom and a better life for your children—every day I wake up thinking about how lucky I am and how grateful and proud I am of your achievements. I thank you for your unconditional love and support, and I am always in your debt.

I am humbled always by the many struggles of LGBTQIA+ activists; it is a long, enduring history and a constant uphill climb for the rights and freedoms we enjoy today, and I hope future generations continue this tradition.

To the amazing team at Duet Books and Interlude Press, thank you for taking a chance on my story. Annie, Candy and Lex—your passion is an inspiration, and your constant support during this process has been absolutely wonderful. This book would not be here without you.

Thank you to Arnab, Becky and Noemie for reading the first draft; your insights and suggestions made the story all the better. Thank you Tiffany, Jeremiah and Leonard for your brilliant work in helping create an amazing trailer for this novel. Jennifer, Kate and Charm—your steadfast friendship means the world to me and I will always be grateful for your energy and positivity, for being there for me and fielding so many strange questions at many an odd hour. Mai, Laura, Cal, Kelly Ann and Stacey, you inspire me and keep me striving to be better. And of course, endless thanks to Niamh, for inspiring me to write again.

Freck, Michelle, Em, Maggie, Mel, Tay, Dani, Beth, Rachel— amazing writers, and even more amazing friends—our little sprinter's circle has grown from just a writer's resource to a source of steady friendship. Thank you so much for the countless moments of laughter and joy, the support and the love; I would not be the person I am today without you.

Last, but never least, for everyone who started this journey with me, those who read my early works and encouraged me, you will always be my anchor.

About the Author

C.B. LEE IS a bisexual writer, rock climber and pinniped enthusiast based in California. She is a first-generation Asian American and has a BA in sociology and environmental science, which occasionally comes in handy in her chosen career, but not usually. Lee enjoys reading, hiking and other outdoor pursuits. *Seven Tears At High Tide* is a first novel.

You can connect to C.B. at cb-lee.com and on Twitter at @author_cblee.

Questions for Discussion

1.   How does Kevin's relationship with Miles affect his feelings for Morgan? How would their relationship have progressed differently without that in Kevin's past?

2.   How does being a halfling change the way Morgan thinks about humans? About himself?

3.   How does Kevin's family and his background help him understand what it was like to be a halfling?

4.   How would Morgan have behaved differently on his mission if he had known from the beginning about the choice he would have to make on his birthday? Would he have allowed himself to become so attached to Kevin if he had thought he'd never see him again after that summer?

5.   How is love different between selkies and humans? Which way is better, in your opinion?

6.   Nathaniel (Nate) appears throughout the story. What do you think were the ethics violations that caused him to lose his funding? How did his character reveal itself as the story went on?

7.   Living without his father wasn't as traumatic for Morgan as it often is for human kids. What about selkie culture makes that possible?

8.   Why was Floyd so willing to believe Morgan was his son, despite never having seen him before?

9.   The idea of humans controlling selkies by hiding their pelts so they can't transform keeps coming back, over and over, in the story. Despite being hurt by that behavior so much in her own life, Linneth eventually tells Kevin to do it to Morgan. Why did she ask that of him? How might the story have been different if Kevin had taken her advice?

10. In Chapter 17, Kevin wishes for Morgan to return. Do you think that had an impact on the story? Why or why not?

11. What was Linneth's role in the boys getting their happily ever after?

—AC Holloway

Say hello to

duet
an imprint of interlude **press**

Summer Love edited by Annie Harper

These short stories are about the emergence of young love—of bonfires and beaches, of the magical in-between time when young lives step from one world to another, and about finding the courage to be who you really are, to follow your heart and live an authentic life.

The contributing authors have written stories about both romantic and platonic love featuring characters who are gay, lesbian, bisexual, transgender, pansexual and queer/questioning. The authors also represent a spectrum of experience, identity and backgrounds.

ISBN 978-1-941530-36-8

The Rules of Ever After by Killian B. Brewer

The rules of royal life have governed the kingdoms of Clarameer for thousands of years, but Prince Phillip and Prince Daniel know that these rules don't provide for the happily ever after they seek. A fateful, sleepless night on top of a pea under twenty mattresses brings the two young men together and sends them on a quest out into the kingdoms. On their travels, they encounter meddlesome fairies, an ambitious stepmother, disgruntled princesses and vengeful kings as they learn about life, love, friendship and family. Most of all, the two young men must learn to know themselves and how to write their own rules of ever after.

ISBN 978-1-941530-35-1

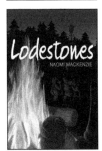

Lodestones by Naomi MacKenzie

On the eve of a new school year, several groups of college students cross paths on their way to a secret end-of-summer lake party, including two inseparable best friends who discover over the course of 24 hours that their relationship is something much deeper than friendship.

ISBN 978-1-941530-37-5

duetbooks.com
the **young adult** imprint of interlude**press**

CPSIA information can be obtained
at www.ICGtesting.com
Printed in the USA
LVHW050033020219
606177LV00018B/232/P